BURN
your
belongings

DAVID
hoenigman

art by
YASUTOSHI
yoshida

BURN your
belongings

DAVID
hoenigman

art by
YASUTOSHI
yoshida

Jaded Ibis Press
sustainable literature by digital means.™
an imprint of Jaded Ibis Productions U.S.A.

To Mayumi

"There is something in me which
simply makes it impossible for
me to accept my lot as it is; I
am cursed with a preposterous
discontent."
                    – Vincent van Gogh

I need to sleep. I can't. the anger I feel overwhelms me. is more than I can deal with. I need to get past him. each time I begin to dream he's there at the threshold. I retreat in fear. he may make even greater demands. awake I'm less at risk. he won't return again until late tomorrow morning. I stare at the ceiling. I listen to the downpour. then it's total darkness. then it's him. he's burrowed himself within and is waiting impatiently. I can feel him pacing in the pit of my stomach. soft hollow echoing footsteps rise up to my ears. something spreads to my chest. downward into my thighs. I understand her desperation now. why she felt she had to give in. my entire body aches. all that has thus far steadied me has collapsed. all that has held me in place. their faces approach and retreat before my eyes. nothing can stop this. it won't be distracted by hope or logic. I'm glad I was able to add to his frustration. that I'm the reason he has nowhere to sleep tonight. I'm happy it's pouring rain. that he must be growing angrier with each puddle he steps into. he caused her to doubt me. what we have is delicate. I fear something like this could make her change her mind. she expects me to defend him. I need her. I could never move forward. until he came I couldn't see this. I only meant that when he wasn't looking or speaking there were moments of tenderness between her and me. moments I knew I'd been forgiven. I need this to calm me. is he capable of sympathy. if I ask forgiveness will the guilt go away. why do I feel guilt if I don't feel sorry. can he exact revenge. would he. has he softened. has he realized it's behind us. it can never be undone. I had good intentions. the things I'm most proud of are trifles. he hasn't disguised this. he took what was his. packed it all into a bag. he kept my umbrella. he's soaked to the bone. now he's turning his back. each step makes him smaller. he's crossing the bridge. soon entirely gone. out of my life. as if he were dead.

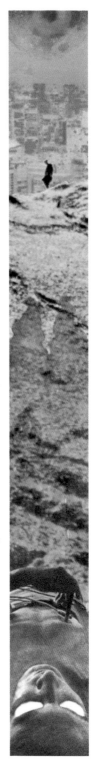

I live near a river. it's too wide to be called a canal. over it extends the bridge that I cross when leaving each morning. that I cross again each night as I'm returning home. the water's filthy. of great interest to her. if she sees something new forgotten there or another dead fish. she can't wait to tell me. almost the first words that come to her mouth in the time we have alone. I knew it was very late. but seeing his light on I hesitantly knocked on his door. I hear his voice from the other side. I have nowhere else to turn. I expected the light that escapes beneath the door to be extinguished. unanswered. sounds of someone walking away. but now we're bathed in it. and I'm apologizing. almost moved to tears. is there more to him. would he chase me away if he thought things would escalate. a part of me I cannot change. I move too slowly. days pass by. I'd sink even lower if I knew it'd make him happy. should this laziness be punished. what if we get hopelessly lost. what if it starts to rain. he'd resent me. he looks hungry. thinks how I've failed him. he's buried up to his neck. his arms pinned to his sides. they're taking little bites. all he can do is squirm. of what other foolishness has he managed to convince her. no wonder they're smiling. whispering into each other's ears. this is the story of this scar. what she believes. what she says prayers to. we'll never again be lonely. I don't understand why he's afraid. I won't fully recover. it descends on me if my hands are idle. is he just tired. is he really this unhappy. I stand on my tiptoes and peek in through the window. he's lying in bed. he looks like a corpse. the empty containers that surround him could be flowers left by mourners. the last glimpse I'll have before they shovel on the dirt. his life's been one mistake followed by another. finally he moans. now he sits up. he doesn't know what he's feeling yet. it's better for me if he still feels lost. when he's hopeful I pity him. I pity us both.

10

I lead him away from there. we sit together quietly. she's broken promises. I still follow her. I see our shadows lifeless on the surface of the water. I stare inside them. there's movement underneath. breathing in and out. confiding in me. I don't remember what it was that made me so reluctant. even if I try I can't see traces of it now. has this strengthened me. has it hollowed me out. have there been other eyes on her. are we not so isolated. her heart's beating fast. she's waiting on the train platform. does he fully understand what he's attempting to justify. I walk past it everyday. I feel its breath. it's late. she's sleepy. tells him a lie so he'll let her leave. I tap on it with affection and hear the empty sound it makes. the way she's molded him. I wasn't looking. I dig in my pockets. now she's left. there's a hole. I throw myself into it. there's nothing worth keeping secret. I open my mouth. he's speaking to me. repeating himself again and again. now's my chance. I have her attention. I'm expecting someone. I have trouble sleeping. I'm ashamed by almost everything and everyone I see. I'm standing too close. I'm afraid of failing. I'm imagining this. I'm still where fear has rooted me. it's a sunny afternoon. I've been waiting all morning. I'm trying to write someone a letter. I'm saving my appetite. I eat a little bread but I want to eat more. I'm crumbling up a sheet of paper. I wonder what she'll wear today. I'm writing him a letter because he sent me a painting. I'm staring at it. I want to feel more than I do. I imagine the arms moving. I imagine it speaking. the kind of voice it'd have. where he'd be standing. in the corner. away from the window. it exceeds my expectations. perhaps not all he's touched has withered. says stupid things. talks in his sleep. he's dishonest. I've never seen him happy. what will she want to eat today. what reason will she give for having kept me waiting. the eyelids of everything heavy but mine.

11

She's childlike. she's lost there. the next day wouldn't get out of bed. they'll all look down on me. the hours won't pass if I think of him. I'll dangle from the lowest branch. I'm growing suspicious. there are things I don't tell her about him. I follow it up narrow steps. it leads me through a door. I have no control over this. I belong to someone. I hate it here. but is it worse than anywhere else. what if it's better. what if I leave and regret it. if I want to come back but I can't. I feel sorry for him but he expects too much from me. I don't want to talk to him anymore today. but he's here. so I have to. I pretend there's nothing bothering me. I know he's not wrong. that he just does what he feels he needs to. a curse that has been cast on him and what he hopes will take her place. to emerge holding hands. had been in there for hours. I'll keep her in the dark. expected something warm and soft. only feel coldness. reach further. fantasize about their deaths. what was on my mind as I passed beneath the bridge. the effect it'd have on me. I can finally give up hope. I'll no longer be indebted. sometimes I catch him sleeping. leaning all the way back in his chair. drool on the corner of his mouth. how it feels when it's forced on me. could she've been poisoned. is it beginning to burn. they are separate. they are miserable. I feel victorious. I don't intervene. there's no need to. he ties the blindfold on himself. he stands up straight. he waits. the night is progressing. she isn't herself. she wonders if to him this constitutes devotion. if he'll ever be capable of more. he wants to celebrate. I'm so proud I can burst. I've too much to tell her. I can't let her sleep. I return home. they've abandoned me. the spare key is missing. I consider breaking the glass. how could there've been a misunderstanding. we spoke just yesterday. I'm exactly on time. it begins to rain. I find shelter. I'll wait. it's not like them not to have left a note on the door.

12

I embarrass her. I could easily walk away. if I never tell a soul. if I insist on its dignity. we've gone beyond this. either she stays or she doesn't. I want to tear it from him. examine it closely until it makes some sense. why doesn't he care what happens to himself. why has he dragged me into this. sits close enough to see the tiny beads of sweat. how I first noticed her. I was near the back. from here it sounds like a whisper. has she just said my name. she knows he's here. she won't give him the satisfaction of trying to avoid him. it feels like we're stuck in this afternoon. like it's lasted days. I want to break his nose. I want the blood to flow down the front of his shirt. I want her to see the look on his face as he's out cold on the floor. would this change things. would he still deserve her affection. even in this weakened condition I could bat him aside like a pesky fly. he never stops talking. it doesn't make sense to me. I'm only watching. and listening as one would to the sound of a train passing. I fall asleep in my shoes and necktie. nothing scares her. I want to see her misery. it's only anger or jubilation. or she complains of being bored. he can't feel sympathy. she recoils. she's hit a nerve. gropes for a near at hand distraction. it's getting cold. gets up. walks across the room. closes the window. so this is what made him flee. what keeps him away still. explains the shape he has assumed. and why he clings to everything I'd hoped he would abandon. now it's mine. like having a child. it's smiling. it's feigning ignorance. it's pretending to have faith in me. I've become protective. I don't trust anyone. she once again loses her patience. I panic. I fear for the illusion I've so carefully watered and fed. it'd break my heart. she'd think I'd caved in. can I bring myself to speak to her lovingly. look in her eyes. convince her there's something that unites us. I'm only avoiding hardship. she wants purpose. she wants even greater obstacles to overcome.

13

I feel relieved when the day passes. closer to somewhere where less is expected. I've failed. I'm left alone. I don't want to think. I don't want to worry. I try again to write him a letter. are things the same. can I show my face there. what would they think of her. is this mild by comparison. should I envy him. is this how he's always seen it. skies blue and cloudless. does it exist elsewhere. has something followed me. do I have any control over it. could I've left it behind. I'll beg her to take me seriously. the hairs are standing up on my arms. the words and deeds of yesterday were those of a stranger. I've now reclaimed what was lost. I'll no longer disappoint her. he sways too easily. I hear her voice from here. she knows I'm listening. I've stopped breathing. he startled me. I spill the cup all over my papers. he says I look worried. have they begun to treat him differently. I hope he doesn't think that it's entirely my fault. I can pinpoint when the change occurred. when whatever it had been had started to dim. is there any trace of me there. does it still inspire feeling. he'll stop her tonight as she's halfway out the door. she'll look at her watch. she'll exhale noisily. he'll wish it were important. he'll rummage through his desk. turn everything upside down. do anything to stall her. he knows I'm waiting downstairs. he knows we think he's a fool. I make them laugh. she can't see that I've progressed. like she has her eyes closed. I dreamt that up until now we'd all been wearing masks. at the end she took hers off. the same greed and cunning. the same selfish reasons. he didn't smile once. should I fear for my safety. would I feel it anyway if he knocked in my teeth. she takes and treasures what was more mine than hers. I knew it was coming. I'd sensed it. she meant for him to run away. to let it sink in. to see that there was no sense in groveling. I'd meant nothing. I'm weak. I'm cowardly. I understand now. time passes. we're alone in a hallway.

14

Everything around us is dying. she looks healthy. he's nervous. he trails off. she's the youngest of them. he's not the only one in love with her. it was easy for her to make this decision. she's noticed the discoloration. she's spent hours with nothing to look at but him. she fears what she can't change. what she can't drape something over. anything that has begun to wonder what it deserves. something I'd hung on the wall fell down. it woke me from a trance. it's lying on the floor. I won't be here much longer. something unforeseen will step forward. will finally show me mercy. this is how I chose to adorn my little pulse today. this is what I've let myself become. I put on my shoes. I step out. I turn and lock the door. I walk down the stairs. I'll be early. I have time to kill. I pause on the bridge. I look for fish. anything floating. I cross to the other side where an old man lives. he walks slowly down his front steps. turns and slowly back up them. turns and slowly down again. over and over. I've seen this before. what he does to keep his blood moving. never looks up. I wonder how old he is. how he deals with the boredom. I have no direction. I'll resist. I'll draw a line here. but life is long. today is inconsequential. she doesn't listen very closely. I'd still like to do the things we'd planned. to her it doesn't matter. if he's sitting with me and we have nowhere to go I still feel happy. if we run out of money. if the rain keeps us inside. I don't feel a loss. I don't feel letdown. she tells me I shouldn't be ashamed. it's only her. it wouldn't stain. that's why I stayed so long. that's how I kept dry. I have nothing to do. I'm staring at the wall. I heard his footsteps just in time. perhaps he'd entered once. saw me sleeping at my desk. left and approached more noisily to save me the embarrassment. it was just that I could so distinctly hear the rain outside. as if I knew where each drop was landing. soon my neck wouldn't hold up my head. soon I ceased to exist.

15

I'm usually able to look busy. I usually have nothing to hide. it's only after hours of loneliness. days since I've seen her last. I curse her under my breath then pounce as she's approaching. I wrap around her tightly. I kiss her cheek. to me it all seems honest. able to coexist. he's excited about something. I can't understand but nod in agreement. I want it to enter into me. to push the other things aside. hoping for this exhausts her. has he noticed me shivering. why won't I speak up. I want to go home. something similar to fear set in before I left this morning. would I do something that would alter things. would my impatience boil over. would what is inside finally rise to the surface. must I respond to this unhappiness. is there a choice. what outward form will it take. what lingers after the colors and shapes have disappeared. who was there. what was said to me. I walk past doorways. I'd rather be going anywhere else. I get on the train. I look at the man across from me. he makes it worse. I suspect he believes everything he was told. that he sees within it dignity. it's almost effortless. has she been honest. do her demons only attack from without. stays in her room until she can't ignore her hunger. it's cold outside. the wind stings her cheeks and ears. I'll be presentable for the hours that it's necessary. afterward I'll step again into a numbing soothing fog. I see her from my window. she's crossing the bridge. she's thinking of turning back. I never know how to respond to this. his unconvincing smile. I worry what he'll say next. what else I'll have to swallow. I wish she were better company. sits quietly. she never asks for anything. she never insults me. I think of the first few awkward moments we spent together. how different it was from what she'd hoped. I've no right to assume she's as spineless as I am. I thought just then her eyes would thank me. that she'd see beyond a doubt I'd not led her astray.

16

She yawns. am I wrong about other things. they must swarm to him each time he wanders from safety. it's left marks on my skin. he won't tell me what's wrong. it's hard not to feel like I've failed him. someone's knocking. it's soft. I imagine the tiny fist of a child. I figure he'll grow tired or bored. go on his way. but it hasn't stopped. it hasn't grown weaker or louder. I try to drown it out. I'm curious. I pause. it's still there. what can be his intentions. what does he want with me. I won't allow him to win. I'll wait it out. I rearrange the room. I throw old things away. is it some duty I'm neglecting. what I've been letting starve. she breathes life into him. is he being rewarded. has he done something to put her at ease. I'll never know what's at the root of it. do I need to. are these its last flickers. am I standing in its way. she seems disappointed that the damage isn't worse. is impressed by their cunning. sees herself in these cowards. what's been withheld. is it this simple. I keep silent because I fear their scorn. it's winning me over. it's eaten who I am. will she view this as a promise. had I hoped she would. something we can cling to when we've bored ourselves to tears. I spin with envy at the way their mouths hang open. banish these thoughts. what's in his heart is wrong. what passes through my mind. what's growing in her. what was contagious. the urgency she feels lately first thing as she wakes. what will I do with all this time. days separate us from there. I'm surrounded by things I no longer want a part of me. drawers full of it. things I'd forgotten. I can't move without turning one over. at times I panic. I'll melt alongside them into the floorboards. I just need to be patient. I just need to try to rest. he can't comfort her. she sees how flimsily it's all held together. I look upon her with a mixture of guilt and triumph. she slides dandelions through her buttonholes. she laughs and enjoys the afternoon. I didn't known then that she'd leave.

17

She's lifted a great weight off my shoulders. she should never have come. as soon as it gets dark I'll drift off unnoticed. they've blurred into one. I can't tell them apart. which elbows are his. which wrists are hers. both in similar colors. she was on his mind all day. swirling beneath the blindfold. I was dizzy. I fell. she's talking about the future. I'm an act of desperation. she's pretending to be fooled. I step toward it. I feel I have to. I was chosen for this. it's unalterable. I'll go with her if she wants to come. if not I'll go alone. he doesn't fight against it. we're saying good night. he doesn't want to leave. he waits until the last second. until he hears the train pull in. then he hurries up the steps. he's speeding past buildings. he's looking out the window. I'm entitled to nothing. none of this is mine. nor will it ever be. I'm getting old. it's too late. I can't make up for lost time. she adds to the pressure. I'll be the reason she suffers. he gets home. goes to bed. the next day's sunny. a butterfly enters through the window. it eludes me. rejoices out of reach. I leave it there. something to greet me when I return. I go with her. it's the first time. children are dipping butterfly nets in the water. we've spent an hour together. we're sitting on a bench. we feel so far from what worries us. we're safe. we're content. I've accepted some of the blame. I try to let it slide off me. I try to carry something of it through to the next day. I'm at work. I'm doing my job. they're all pores of the same skin. slight differences. I'm beginning to be able to tell them apart. a place is readied for her. she's exceptional. he'll be completely forgotten. I discover something new every day. a quicker way to get to the train station. a new outlook. he crowds me. he wants to get past. throw himself at her feet. rid me of everything. drain me of this tainted blood. all of it connects. why what he had blew away. sticks to nothing. owes him nothing. would never fight to keep him.

He was waiting for me below in the street. I shouldn't assume I've made him feel privileged. doesn't he have what he wants. hasn't it ended happily. am I trying too hard to see a difference. is any of this real. have I found someone I can trust. why am I taking it so lightly. she says I'm obsessed with guilt. I'll never relinquish it. I believe it will someday lead me some place livable. that it will look good from afar. I didn't have to earn this. it spilled forth from her. it wants me this way. it's patient for now. it tucks me in tenderly. it speaks sincerely. I'll lower my voice. we have time. we have hope. we're better off than the others. he tries to downplay what it's meant. how it's changed things. I grab them one by one by their hair and drag them out. they don't fight. they sit there shivering and bewildered. I slam the door on their faces. they've only ever known comfort here. they've grown fat and soft off me. they're too shocked to protest or appeal to my loyalty. now I only have her. I wish I could choose what she'd say next. decide exactly when it should fade. who should survive this. who benefits. is it a second childhood. should I decline this type of safety. she's left little wet footprints. I'd meant well then. I was still trying to slap myself awake. I squeeze her wrist. I'm holding her beating heart. it's throwing doors open. it's ripping down curtains. uncertain steps forward. finally life in their eyes. looking untrustingly at their hands in the sunlight as if they were miracles performed by a god that they'd scorned. I lean closer to her. I want to hear what she's whispering. someone shares my name here. someone shares my fingerprints. strands of my hair. I don't claim to be anyone. I want nothing for myself. I want to be absorbed by this. disintegrate inside it. is she asking this of me. is it worth what she's sacrificed. my vision clears. I worry he doesn't sleep enough. I won't be happy until it costs me something. until I die and begin anew.

19

She thinks she's trapped. I listen intently every time she makes a wish. I'll somehow see to all of them. even the ones she's forgotten. the mornings will be so different then. we'll move as slow as turtles. it'll be almost totally quiet. only our breathing. we'll eat like kings. until we're bursting. we'll forget this completely. what we do without now. what makes us so tired. I leave the lights off as the sun's setting. until the darkness claims this room. puts me at peace. he isn't with me now. it's my chance to dissect this. what he thought was harmless. hopefully it escapes him. or he attributes it to something else. I wonder what awaits me. calls in sick. falls back asleep until the late afternoon. it's raining again. it rains too much here. the wind blows it sideways. an umbrella does little good. I eat my dinner dripping wet alone in a cheap restaurant. couldn't this form of solace suffice. wouldn't I miss this tranquility. there's no sense in waiting until I'm dry. it's still raining just as heavily. I return home. someone new's moved in. he mumbles a greeting then pulls his door shut. I lay on my back and watch her dripping from the ceiling. she's radiant. we've been arguing. I realize now that I was wrong. that I spoke without thinking. she's at work. he knocks then opens the door. he comes in. he turns the lights on. our eyes adjust. he'd thought of an excuse in the hallway. a reason to be here. he begins speaking. whatever it is falls apart in the air. he leaves without closing the door. she sees it all one color. everyone partially to blame. have I come to my senses. have I forgiven him too readily. he's looking in the mirror. she knows everything about me. even what I've never told her. she listens in on my dreams. I'll go there now. I'll meet her in the street on her way home. she'd never expect that. we could go somewhere together. I see her shape approaching. it's my responsibility. she's walking around puddles. she's looking at her feet.

20

She stares at him. we haven't really known each other very long. she wants him to talk. wonders what he's willing to admit to. I thought that something I'd done had made this impossible. I wasn't asking to be rescued. I've enjoyed myself. I see faces everyday. teeth. frowns. glasses. skin. eyes blinking. which ones have voices. which ones need sleep. food. warmth. in the afternoon when nothing's hiding. she's blocking her ears. she collapses in my arms. all of them are dripping. muttering. walking around in circles. each day I check the mailbox. each day it's empty. no one ever misses me. I hope I never even cross their minds. what he's mistaken her friendliness for. what I could see instantly. she opens her mouth. he's almost on top of her. I followed him because I didn't know anyone else. because I needed somewhere to go. I snuck away when he wasn't looking. became curious. turned around. I'm watching him from a distance. joyously in and out of these doors. armfuls more of it. he looks like a snail suddenly ripped from its shell. how long will he wait for me. people are buying flowers. waiting in line at the bakery. talking to each other. he's the only one doing nothing. he's the only one I recognize. he stands where he thinks he'll be most visible. then moves to a different spot. then he walks away. then he returns. he looks angry. I laugh to myself. I drift into the crowd. she must have left. I've been foolish. was there a reason. was there something I should've been able to sense. everything is growing stronger or weaker. or disappearing from sight. all that's scattered around him. what puts smiles on these faces. he reaches for something to steady himself. I expect them to provide for me. I'm a speck on this. I keep hoping one will spring to life. I'm emptied of all but envy. I'm at home again. I'll go days without speaking. I've caught a cold. I take a tissue. I blow my nose. I squeeze it into a ball. I add it to a pile of them.

21

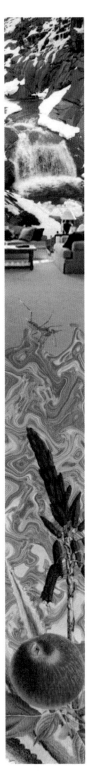

He throws open the curtain and lets in the moonlight. he looks around the room with satisfaction. I've finally achieved some semblance of order. I've tucked everything away. afterward. think of consequences. twists around me. the ugly spin I could put on this. I lower myself into it. he doesn't give me what I want. it's forced me to continue with greater urgency. it flutters away. settles in blackness. I kill it. smear it into the cheap carpet. hit it again. I'm still afraid that when I leave to get a dustpan it'll roll over on its legs. be on its way. I was testing her. I didn't care whether or not she was sleeping. I wanted her to hear. I wanted her to know for once how I really feel. that I'm not kind. that I don't like any of these people. she rolls over. there's nothing to hope for with him. today he listened. only a few minutes. it almost never happens. I've attached more meaning to it than it deserves. like all things. what I commemorate. what I insist owes me its love. only scenery. hollow on the inside. held up with wires. it can wait until tomorrow. she's determined to get some sleep. I don't care that we've been lied to. I don't share his sense of defeat. how it's crept into almost everything he says. how it prevents him from being happy. I did this in her honor. I want her to feel loved. I want us to feel peace. I savor every word she says. it may be weeks before I hear her voice again. some of them put me at ease. some of them fill me with dread. will she have time for me. it gives me chills. I hold my breath. I thought I hadn't dropped a single crumb. somewhere I went wrong. somewhere my attention slipped. I've been spared any real tragedy. only things in my way. things half completed. I'm lying on the grass. she's next me. she's telling me something. I'm staring up at the clouds. I'm thinking about him. about how he'd think I was lazy. I could live with much worse. all desire leaks out of me. soaks into the ground.

He never seems to waste a moment. I don't like to have to rely on him. but I need a favor and he has an overabundance of everything. would he notice if something were missing. could I accept charity. which would eat at me worse. which would stick to me longer. she's stubborn. she won't share this joy. thinks she knows what they are going to say before they open their mouths. I've made everything bow to this. it'd be easy to make peace. to ease us all into relief. to heal in this surrender. am I the only one who remembers her. where she usually sat. how her soft voice would drown all else out. make the evenings tolerable. what had been somewhere just to kill the hours. a place to sit until I needed to be somewhere else. he's still impressionable. changes slightly from week to week. I want what they have. I want to understand what they're saying. it isn't admiration. it's a need to do penance. to protect myself against being passed over. none of this ever happened. it seems to me now. but if I had imagined it why wasn't it perfect. why didn't it obey me. give me even the smallest compliment. hold open doors. when he finally gets here. the few moments that are mine. his eyes are half closed. he can't string together words. can't tell me where he's been. the next morning I sail up the stairs and burst into the room. she sees it all days before it happens. how it starts. how it ends. she digests it. she waits. she's making threats. it's a fraction of what it should be. as is his regret. and how much he cares. and what he has to give. and the least she should accept. I can't let her know that I have nowhere else to go. she'd hold it over me. she thinks I never worry. that I'm missing something. that no one could ever keep a secret from her. she enters without making a sound. I was thinking about what I was going to say to her. then she's standing right in front of me. expecting something. as if I'd called her. I can't explain anything. I don't know where to begin.

These rooms are too small. I can't even stretch. everything is old and falling apart. anyone who's ever lived here must've been unhappy. she searches each morning for the smallest indication as to the nature of the coming day. the weather. how long it takes her to find what she needs. how fast or slowly the few remaining minutes pass. if she has the right change. if she can get a seat on the train. who's sitting across from her. is there something she was meant to see. I don't deserve better. I'm lucky to have anything at all. she listens to me complain until I have nothing more to say. until I can finally begin to relax. I'm not accustomed to such devotion. have I forgotten anything. when she usually gives in. when she says I'm too hard on myself. this will go on forever. he thinks he's busy. thinks there'll be something at the end of it. this is my fault. I shouldn't have fed this. he's trying to appear as if his thoughts are elsewhere. makes what he believes to be a blank face. a face I've tired of looking at. we'll carry on. we'll expect less. he's finally ready for bed. I've been watching him all day long. I imagine this spread thinly for years and years. until a stop is finally put to it. I consider us animals. I allow them to examine a drop of my blood. she won't recognize me. all of us look the same. none of us took pity on her. the first raindrop that landed in her palm. there're still footsteps at this hour. she lays down but isn't tired. if I didn't want more. if I could slow to a crawl. I'm still warmed by this memory. we swam out past everyone. all the way to the boundary. the water was so clear. we could see the sand and rocks far below beneath our feet. someone alone in a small boat fishing. but far enough away. it's rare for her now. not to care. to wander off. I love how it feels afterward. like I'll never have to sleep again. something's stung my arm. the skin on the inside of my elbow begins to bubble. we've returned from where we were.

24

He'd never be able to find his way through these narrow sharp turning streets without her. she's convinced herself that someday he'll gush with gratitude. they look right past me now. even if there's nothing there. an empty corner. a bare wall. I blame everything on her. even what began before we met. I remember her refusal to feign innocence. how it charmed me. now those things are stones I've piled in a place she'd never think to look. things I can someday use against her. I didn't know what brought her there. she watched with some interest. laughed once. I'd learn more. I'd hear it in a steady stream. I never forget the temptations I overcome. they sit together in a dimly lit room and wait for me to beckon them. she must've told dozens of people that she loved them. given them permission to treat her unkind. I could fight against this like I've watched others do. I could refuse to let complacency advance. I'm waiting for her. I'll suck the last bit of her strength. he wants everyone to leave but he can't appear impatient. aspects of him disappoint her. she doesn't know how much worse off he was when he thought that no one cared. I called him a liar though I suspected he was just forgetful. perhaps I overreacted. was alarmed by my own reflection. lashed out at everyone who'd ever stepped on me. made an enemy for no good reason. she's ashamed of this. isn't saying much. tomorrow will be totally different. we'll be alone. we'll be able to hear someone coming from a mile off. he always tries to catch us off guard. when he entered I was perusing the bookshelf. she was working at her desk. she's too smart for him. he gets flustered and becomes clumsy. I leave this behind. I take the train home. I get there. the walls are paper-thin. I overhear her singing to herself. sometimes she leaves the door open a crack. everything looks temporary. she tells them she enjoys being alone. she never has trouble finding him.

25

It's just as hot as yesterday. the day's first drops of sweat are forming on my brow. I'm walking down a hill. he's coming toward me on a bicycle. grimacing from the uphill climb. he sounds like he's dying. he passes. yesterday I suddenly felt homesick. I want to see him. I want to tell him about my life here. at times I forget that we're no longer friends. she turns her shoulders until her spine emits a series of soft cracks. what am I forgetting. someone is waiting for me. I was supposed to bring her something. no attempt is made at beauty. they succeed easily and gloat over their ability to manipulate. he comes home exhausted. sits down at the table. they bend themselves into hideous shapes. I can't wake him from this though I've shaken him gently. I know inside there's kindness. that it's starving. that it's wearing him out to never ask for help. if I left I'd worry about him. someone asks us to lift up our feet and sweeps up the bits of garbage underneath. there are other interruptions. there are plenty of open spaces but he squeezes in next to her. I can be of some use. I can scare away strangers. why did he leave her. they both seemed happy. now they both look lost. it was the only hope I had of winning her affection. I wanted to be mothered. I wanted something that wouldn't run. she should be here like she promised. I don't really care what's on his mind. I want nothing more to do with him. I've been sitting at this desk for hours. as soon as I arrive and sit down I want to leave. but I'm never happy at home. I like being in between. I like walking to and back from the train station. I like being on the train. so many people and none showing any emotion. it's almost unbelievable. it's comforting. I think of never being seen again. of staying here always. never drawing any attention to myself. letting them replace me. watching people that mean nothing to me scatter in all different directions as they reach the bottom of the stairs.

I don't want to begin this. I'm stalling. he quickens his pace. passes two or three people and crosses the bridge. I'm never able to convince anyone of anything because inside I feel I don't deserve their understanding. they must see this. they must think there's no real choice. he doesn't know when to feel safe or how to explain it to her. if only I could gaze at this until my curiosity were satisfied. it seems worse than usual tonight. the streets seem dirtier. I'm moving slower. I stay here to avoid answering questions. she sees a silhouette. it must have sprouted roots. she looks again. he looks at me as if I were a picture hung on the wall. something that wouldn't answer. has she seen us together. I put my head down on the desk and feel a low deep rumble in my stomach. maybe she's right. maybe I'm unhealthy. am I honestly trying. have I fooled myself. am I searching for defeat. do I need it for some reason. he'll be here soon. everything requires effort. I hear them. I want to join them. though her voice is sadly absent. where they look upon her lovingly. laugh knowingly. I stop. I weigh the consequences. if I knew how to give in to whatever it is I was supposed to. if I awoke and saw it clearly. she watches his first childish attempts. how has he survived this long without knowing any better. is it how his face still looks young. he's drifted off again. he's avoiding everyone. she's telling me what she thinks I need. gives me things. an alarm clock. a feather duster. I do exactly as she says. she still doesn't trust me. it's someone else's fault. what she can't imagine life without. they're arguing down the hall. he raises his voice and slams the door. it won't be easy. would she still be recognizable if cured of this. will she ever stop worrying about how it appears. all the other things I ask myself. the day starts perfectly. now it's late afternoon. I have nothing to show for the entire time I've been here. I've wasted years.

27

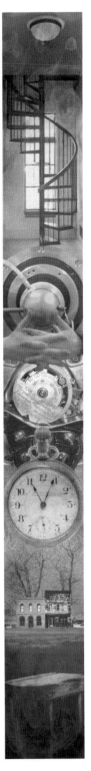

She watches him paint the walls. he doesn't care if he misses spots. fifty years could pass and I'd know him by a glance. he'd be exactly the same. I picture them framed in green leaves and sunshine. pressed to each other. wearing new clothes every day. it's only sadness when compared to this. otherwise it approaches joy. he's the only one I ever wonder about. the rest have never stopped laughing. have petrified somewhere between where I am now and there. I see one with his hand raised about to slap another on the back. the one who's doubled over. forever unaware of what has passed by. we were the same once. what separates me from them now. what gives me this satisfaction. it's the same ignorance. it's how I must look to them. he's given up in frustration. I never should have chosen someone so beautiful. she'd freeze to death just to make me feel sorry for ever bringing her here. I'm turning blue. I'm losing the feeling in my toes. it's a way to not apologize. I'll spoon-feed him. I'll wipe the dribble from his chin. I'll let the accusations echo against the furthest wall. drop harmlessly before they return to us. the way that I first noticed him. what I'm used to now. can withstand without showing discomfort. she's failed in her attempts to make him feel needed. it's certain that I'll suffer but I'll keep what's most sacred out of reach. they are relentless. I find it hard to part with even the most meaningless shred. ideals are foolish he's decided based simply on how she enters a room. I won't be there the next time this little voice calls. I'll get up early tomorrow. I'll miss her. regardless of how she feels. whether or not she thinks of me at all. he's chosen gray. it was the cheapest. it covers everything. makes him appear sensible. makes them feel they're in good hands. I get lucky sometimes. they meet here after dark. he isn't always there to chase them away. he fits the description. hides behind a tree. it's as important as life or death.

28

The day we went there it was raining. I was afraid that he would turn on me. we are trying to understand each other. she's losing sight of this. I'm losing faith in things that she doesn't agree are beautiful. it's hopeless. further away from what had been a possibility. can we recover. will we be happy again. she's gone under. needs to sit down. she emerges. lately it happens almost every day. it's worse than the last time. it passes. we forget about it. I'm making her laugh. all I'm capable of. she squeals with delight as we turn each corner. the glow from the lights turns her face different shades. one then another. this is all laid out before us. she attributes it all to me. he thinks I don't do anything all day. that I just stare out the window waiting for him to arrive. that I can't see beyond this. that I'm forever bent to hear a whisper. as soon as they didn't need me anymore they all scattered. they've forgotten everything I've ever said. something has replaced me in their minds and hearts. has distorted their faces. he watches her preparing dinner. washing the vegetables. placing mismatched lids on simmering pots. her hair's pinned back from her face. she turns toward an open window and fans herself with her hands. she wants him to stay. she hates how still it gets. she won't risk injury. she won't leave herself exposed. it soothes me to witness this decline. I startle her. she lets out a little scream and reaches for the doorknob. we're perfect for each other. I'm wearing the shirt she bought for me. I'd made her a promise. I broke it and pretended it'd slipped my mind. I knew what I was doing. I knew what she'd think. it lasts such a short time. he'd meant it when he said it. I believed him. I got lost this morning. everything looked different. I thought I knew where I was going. I'll be late. I'll miss my opportunity. she's waiting for the light to change. she's a shadow of it. it's uneven. none of us are any better. what she still feels she needs.

29

I didn't hear a sound or would've gotten out of bed to say goodbye. I know exactly why he doesn't like me. the life he's breathed into this shell. I want isolation. I never have time. I have dozens of excuses. she walks down the street imagining she's being watched from every window. she's just as he'd described her. it's exhausting. I'll get under her skin. I don't need encouragement. what she lives for. what brings life to her eyes. he thinks I never dream. that this is all I want. that this won't eventually evaporate. I wanted to show her the spot in the river where three bicycles were rusting just below the surface of the water. suddenly I couldn't handle being alone. it still plagues her. I'm sitting in a waiting room. I'm watching people in pajamas. with crutches. with canes. with braces strapped around themselves. moving slowly and unhappily in and out of doors. she returns sooner than I'd expected. we move to another room and wait for someone else. I want to say something but I can't. everything I think of I reject as insensitive. we leave. there's almost nothing to worry about. we can talk about anything. it doesn't have to be this. she could save me so easily. I need to find somewhere else to live. I can hear him blowing his nose late at night. as if he were standing over my bed. I hear everything. they must hear every sound I make. I hope he isn't too exhausted when he arrives. will I have his approval. I'll never turn back then. she can't wait to see him again. it's worth the sadness he causes. her eyes are needy and threatening. he's a safe distance away. he hides behind something whenever I turn around. he's too fast. I never see him. if it wasn't for the weather nothing would ever change. even then the difference is slight. it's getting closer. it's what always runs through my head upon hearing such news. they stopped us as we were leaving. it was me she'd meant to approach. it always is. he stood in between us. I left empty-handed.

30

If they're there. if I've given life to them. are they collected somewhere. will I be punished. is something I can't communicate with laughing at me. what birds chirping really are. or snippets of conversation I happen to overhear. or pages I never open to. I envy their dedication. pushed and pulled by certainty. I can see the lights from the hotels and hear the trains. I can see in all their windows. they're relaxing in almost the same way. black shadows followed by smaller gray ones. at that moment he could have struck her. he was afraid he'd lose his balance. tumble helplessly and splash somewhere below. I wrote the names of everyone I knew on a sheet of paper and began crossing certain ones off. when the paint begins to peel. when those that felt they had a choice have not been seen in years. she'll still care. of this I'm certain. if she doesn't accept this excuse he'll instantly make another. then another. until the daylight dwindles. he never answers when I knock. he must know it's me. am I the only one who ever comes to him. does he know anyone else. she'd know if I needed her. she'd somehow hear me. I miss everything that has passed. I distrust every action meant to take what is there away and replace it with something foreign. something new. I still dream of people I've long since lost contact with. they act as if it'd been a misunderstanding. the initial shine has worn off. I no longer notice the small things. I try to behave as she expects. someone's stolen it. it was here this morning. if he's still alive. if there are others around him. do they hassle him. do they not allow him to grow. if he saw me he'd ignore me. there's nothing I can give him now. he looks long and deeply at his reflection. what inspires such harsh criticism. I make thousands of wishes every day. this is the only one that ever came true. I saw her again. she entered one afternoon. confidently. as if she'd been expected.

31

It's so quiet in here. it's just like my bedroom. the time I spent with him he was always angry. perhaps he's better now. I'll never tell her. it'd only alarm her. it'd make it more difficult for her to relax. he beats himself senseless before he tries to sleep. I need strength. today was unbearable. I see stars beneath my eyelids. they begin to resemble her. I want a glass of water. I shouldn't get up. my blood would circulate. I'd be wide-awake. where has he hidden them. I need certainty. I need to know what he thinks I'm incapable of. I can steal. I can be as quiet as a mouse. I move down the stairs and out the door. I turn the corner. couples are embracing underneath their umbrellas. I can't tell by looking at them which ones are happy. which ones trust each other. I remember the last time. just after the sun had risen. she's hungry and thirsty. she's waiting upstairs for me. I dodge raindrops. inside it's dry. I can take my wet shoes off. it comforts me to think of her as a stranger. detached. not entitled to anything more than this. if he could see me now he'd be proud. even he would envy this level of pleasure. it's a celebration of having successfully disappeared. of how far away I've run. all this temporarily covers what's real. what's constantly growing uglier. it's not really important to anyone. they have other things on their minds. eventually it'll lose momentum. does she believe even a word of it. has it become too confusing. she may be swept away before I can return. the room may be empty. the reason I was running. what has devoured others may begin beckoning to me and I may be too weak to resist it. no one ever sits in those chairs placed out in the hallway. I feel like they're reserved for someone I've wronged. someone who's been searching for me all this time. who'll be sitting there one morning and expect an explanation. I'll kiss their feet. I'll give them everything I have. I'll survive on bread and water. I just want this feeling to leave.

32

She considers it a little trophy. the first evidence that she's worthy of their attention. I slid it out of my pocket and dropped it into her bag just as she was exiting the train. it was crowded. she was talking with her friends. no one noticed a thing. I want to follow her. see how she responds. but I have to go to work. who can I share this with. having made a difference. being a success. he went home and prepared for the next day. among other things she was expected to digest this. what's unavoidable. what's salivating and moving toward her. can she maintain her dignity. is it right to. can she use this to her advantage. I'm awaiting further instructions. will I be able to see a change tomorrow. will the vulnerability be gone. she sees how helpless he is. wonders if she's chosen hastily. his threats have little impact. she gets up. as if she were sleepwalking takes clothes she hates from her closet and puts them on. she's given me little bits and pieces. I only know how terrible she feels. she's crossing the bridge. I watch her move through the rhythmless patter. I watch her close her umbrella. slip out of her shoes. I see the bumps that make up her spine. I want no part of it. whatever is happening outside. whatever makes her look so afraid. there was an urgency in the way they walked. now he's practically dragging her. the past has vanished. overwhelmed as they are by the present. by the future. again I'm wondering if this anger isn't justified. how they aren't sickened by themselves. I saw something today. they surrounded him and forced him into the back seat of a car. I figured he must have done something foolish. he was much older than them. how do they whip themselves into such a frenzy. he struggled but it was surprisingly quiet. everyone just walked past. I returned to my desk. it hadn't occurred to me to tell the police until much later. until I thought about what others would've done. it's too late now. it's becoming weaker.

33

She's trying to look busy. she smiles as he comes in. she's one of the phantoms. a part of this with little bells tied to it. glows unnaturally. perhaps he was relieved. perhaps he wanted concreteness. she walks out. is the emptiness caused by her absence or something less conditional. something enduring. is she a distraction from it. he watched her eyes grow red and burst. he didn't understand but he'd never hoped to. it's a shame we haven't met until now. with no faith in simplicity. I feel as though I've abandoned something. as if I've become convinced of a lie. will this retain its shape. I look at the clock. why must it always be him. surrounded by the recognizable. knowing the sound everything makes. how it feels against this skin. where it was left. seen last. how much of it was consumed. how much of it waits for me. how old everything is. an idea of where it came from. what space was cleared for it. how we drop at the same speed. how it's my duty to protect it. anything that disagrees with this I dismiss as imagination. a scream I thought I'd heard. but there's no reason to scream. I count the change I have in my pockets. it's exactly the same as before. I count the books on the shelves. I separate the ones I've read from the ones I haven't. I'm the only thing alive in here. I can rip everything to shreds. or set it aflame. once I've altered it. once I've left my mark. it'll never be the same. it's proof that I exist. I've done something to upset her. every time I approach she buries her head. if I were there at the time. if it'd drifted up to me. if both doors were closed could I've heard her. she stares at the pattern on the ceiling. it must be the same in every room. I assumed she'd be safe. that they eat each other alive in places reserved only for them. that it was too far for them to stray. uncovered. exposed to the elements. that they'd burn and turn to ashes before they could even get close. I misunderstood this. she paid for my mistakes.

34

I should've barred the door. I should've tried to entice her. but I wanted it to end. I wanted her to prove me wrong. there's a hush. people who couldn't possibly know this. people who've never seen me before. they sense it on me. the way animals know things. I envied her. she lived in a different world. around me I knew every detail by heart. I was bored to tears. even now she tells me not to worry. even after I'm left with nothing. it's strange to see him here. dressed as he usually is. sulking in the corner. we're being punished for having hope. we're being made examples of. I thought she could float entirely free of this. that I could carry the burden for her. the majority of each day is spent this way. trying not to let her know I'm looking at her. waiting for her to speak. he reacts as if it were some troubling news. something that he can't imagine how he hasn't heard until now. something that must be dealt with at once. how hasn't he felt it. how couldn't he. it was there when I woke up. when I got dressed. when I stepped outside. all the way here. when I arrived and turned the lights on. when I first sat down. what shields him. what cuts him off so completely. I need this. I need to be submerged. he remembers me. he listens. something begins. the reason all of us came here. the room empties. I'm tired of always feeling admiration for others and never receiving any myself. of being happy for their success. of searching for similarities. of wishing things were different. thinking that it's hopeless now. punishment for the sins I committed as a child. it's something stamped on me. it's embodied by anyone that disturbs me in the process. when I hear doors open or bells ring. what they're symbols of. where my attention should be. I clean up after them. I've become this color. my head hurts. I want to be someone else. she looks just like him. like unused parts of him sewn together. the appearance of wanting to be forgotten. of waving a useless magic wand.

I should've fought more. I should've tried to remember more. she feels a tug. her love for him trying to escape. it'll sail upward and away like a balloon whose string has slipped through a child's hand. I'm fortunate. no one ever looks at me. there are pictures on the walls that cover the holes I've made. there's a window with hardly any view. she hopes he doesn't come to see her today. this should hurt him but it doesn't. he beats everything into the same shape. she's all aflutter. it's like I'm slipping into a warm bath. her words are the bubbles. they rejoice in her absence. they occasionally glance out the window to make sure she isn't coming. it'd kill her to smile. she'd feel like she'd given in to them. a cockroach scurries underneath the door and into my room. she screams. it's the biggest one I've ever seen. she tries to kill it. she swings at it with a shoe but misses every time. finally I grab the shoe from her and swing down repeatedly until I hear a crunch. she grabs another shoe and swings down three or four more times in the exact same spot. now she'll never sit still. there may be someone outside looking in. she demonstrates how one could easily slide the frosted glass aside and peek in through the crack. I don't question why he's being so kind. I'm needy and he's willing to provide. he inspects for damages. he's talking to himself. alone on the perimeter. incapable of more. she points everything out to me. there are rusty pipes down there. there are skeletons. she says she feels sorry for the fish. a cold certainty has crept into my heart. she's lying about how she spent her day. is it important that she's trustworthy. not yet. I won't ask questions. if I accuse her she'll be angry regardless of whether or not she's told the truth. I just want to enjoy myself. I want to pretend we've escaped. she removes a pin from her hair and it falls down over her shoulders. he doesn't suspect a thing. I don't feel guilty. both of them need me.

Her voice sounded soft and relaxed as if she were lying in bed. it can fall apart now. I'm muttering. I can withstand this. it's justice. it's what I've always been moving toward. she hates these kinds of streets at night. no lights. no sound. it's late but I haven't eaten. it's a form of discipline. he's leaving soon. part of him has already left. I like saying goodbye to people I know I'll never see again. it reaffirms what I've come to believe. that I was a ghost. that I'll continue to dream and speak far beyond where there's nothing more to see. places only I could inhabit. my face blurred. my eyes a different color. my name forgotten. I ask for her. I'm understood. she's brought forward into the light. she hasn't aged. all of this is mine. everything that was always off limits or hidden behind doors. the sun makes everything glow as I'd willed it. she doesn't understand what her beauty entitles her to. she has no memory of him. he's a shadow that tells lies to other shadows. he'll amount to less than dust. I came upon them sitting on the bridge. she'd been crying. he greets me cheerfully. tries to engage me so that I won't look at her. so that my imagination won't run wild. I've seen enough. every possible solution involves sacrifice. what'll she do. what'll she let go of. I want to sleep until everyone I've ever known has died. those that pretend to be oblivious to my anger. those that await an apology. I miss everything about her. sounds she made. things she did that hurt me. failure grants me certain liberties. I stay in my room where it's silent and shaded. I celebrate each minute that passes. I want evidence to be found. I want something that will change the direction of the tide. place me gently in my previous innocence. before I understood. before I'd turned against them. have I successfully buried everything. am I safe now. I can see the outlines. I can count the ribs. I can piece the rest together. my life is the same as hers. we happily collapse.

37

I dreamt she was here. that I woke up in her arms. the sheets smell like her. everything's changed. everything's calm. someday something will be awakened in him. thus far he has lived a cowardly life. if I understood I'd take the blame for it. I had such hope. it stripped everything of its meaning. made it worthless. I had only to stay alive and wait. gather the scraps that'd been left behind. I've decided this. I must have. who else would have. who wanted this for me. he's so unkind to himself. looks dreadful in the morning. watches others run up and down the steps. do they feel they have control. do they know that what they want will come to them. are they certain of it. I can function despite the dizziness. I arrive before her. I watch from the window as she crosses the street toward our building. she has a different umbrella. I follow him. his breath is strong. I can smell it even from behind. he feels sweat trickling down his spine as he passes the shop windows. he considers reverting to a state that formerly brought happiness. if I turn here. if I let them curse me. where these sudden desires for freedom usually lead. but it ends. and nothing's solved. I'm still in this skin. I still have this responsibility. he's killing the flowers. he's letting the vegetables grow rotten. I look at him closely. is he really a threat to me. he took her from right under my nose. I still haven't learned. it's too late. it's digesting in his intestines. he pats me on the shoulder sympathetically. what they always hide behind. that there are circumstances that make loyalty obsolete. we shouldn't trouble ourselves. we shouldn't pretend that who we were hasn't died. do I unearth them. do I stare until I see faces. things they were afraid to tell me. things that unfold in his mind still today just as clearly as when they'd happened. this isn't fair. we shouldn't allow him to walk away. he's said it. he's done it. we should brand it into his skin.

38

She finds an umbrella on the train platform. she'd forgotten hers. she picks it up. she enters and walks to her desk. he approaches. he's speaking. his eyes are giant. his hands are constantly moving. I nod my head and think of silence. I've never seen him reflective or motionless. is he expressing joy. is he trying to belittle me. is he lonely or bored. he eventually stops. turns. reluctantly leaves. it's almost the end of the day. it's almost the end of the week. I sit in here and hope no one bothers me. I rub my eyes. I walk to the window. I watch people outside. I try to imagine how she must feel. I hate when he comes in without knocking. it means I must always be expecting it. have I come away from this with nothing. it's just luck. it requires nothing. it's the instinct to please others. even less. it's the instinct not to starve. far ahead I see their tiny silhouettes pass beneath the streetlights. I hear each movement. I see them shake with laughter. I need this. I need to be shown its absurdity. she points out the black clouds. something like a weak punch lands in the back of my skull. I step inside her skin. there's nothing to do but stand here. look like we're waiting for something. I pick the petals off her. I notice what I'm wearing. the morning seems like days ago. when I buttoned this shirt. when I tied my shoes. it never was. we were forced together. we were squeezed until we were dry peels. I felt they were attacks against me. she'll be happy despite this. she walks through the unfurnished rooms. a place to start again. a place to be alone. my shadow. the little noise I make. the pressure I feel to decide. she's never been in love. I give and kiss and hold out of fear. I'm imitating something I've seen. how is he different. he isn't. it's an insult. it grows thin. when I've dismissed this. when I see her hurry to and from nowhere. hoping to jog his memory. or has she distorted it. it's a blur of faded colors. it's a nonsensical string of words.

39

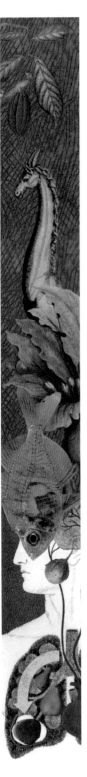

He comforts her as best he can but she never senses any real concern. she wants to know his secret. how he never feels remorse. what he honestly thinks of himself. why it's so easy to condemn her. the sun rises. he lets go of her and she falls. the building spins. the hallway extends into infinity. someone is carrying a young child in their arms. I want to join them. I want to revel in their and my own hopelessness. I give up. I want to be found like this. the noise is driving me crazy. in and out of his room dozens of times an hour. someone's snoring. she left a half full glass on his desk. he left it there for days. until just before he knew she'd come again. then poured it down the drain. she hasn't seen yet. she doesn't know how much I hate confusion. who'll take the blame for this powerlessness. looks up at me coldly. there's an element of truth in what she said. I decided to buy her a present. I don't want to lose her. I couldn't find anything I was certain she'd like. I went home. she's in the other room. I want something else to occupy my mind. but it keeps returning. it'd be the end of us. she turns on the lights and walks to the dresser. she knows they all think she's foolish. why do they respond like this. why do they grin from ear to ear. she's asked a question. she's expected to hide her bitterness. I'm delighted she's failed so miserably. I knew a thick fog would roll in and make them seem to disappear. he can't believe his luck. he hurriedly digs his keys from his pocket and unlocks the door. they stagger in before him. this has become her entire existence. waiting to see to what extremes his loneliness would drive him. it's familiar. it's consistent. it's better than having no one to talk to. above someone is pacing. someone runs up the stairs and arrives out of breath. what is it this time. have they been talking to her again. he'll have to calm her down. brush her lovingly under his wing. afterward it'll feel wrong. weeks will go by.

40

My muscles are still sore. he didn't notice he'd cut his ear. there was a crash. almost everyone was afraid to turn and look. he wants to fight. I'm watching the blood gather in the hollow of his collarbone. the sweat on his forehead. the stupidity in his eyes. it's still early in the evening. from a certain angle she loses her identity completely and becomes an amalgamation of all those I've seen passing beneath my window. he'll never recover in time. puts on a fresh bandage. I wrap my arm around her. he hasn't even noticed. he presses me up against a wall. he bores me to tears. I push his mouth away. it's time I was honest. I close my eyes and see her. a conversation we'd had years ago. she's fidgeting. she's playing with the rings on her fingers. all of it I've heard before. listening exhausts me. acting concerned. speaking for him. telling her what he may be thinking. what this could mean. I can't allow my eyes to drift downward. I can't give further credence to what she already suspects. I've seen how little mercy is shown them. but how does this appear. what would anyone assume. I remind myself that I'm imaginary. that I'm made up of magic dust. that none of this belongs to me. that this room is only used for storage. that I'm only temporary. a bridge people walk across to get to each other. an ear. something to look at. I bring my sadness to her. I make her feel generous. patient. another lifetime goes by. I must go through childhood again. I must be reintroduced to her. I must rejoice the first time she calls me by name. I want to get closer. know every hope and fear. anticipate her little quirks. all that lies hidden beneath what she presents in the daytime. this is her voice. her smell. I'm not mistaken. if anyone should know it's me. these are my secrets. this is what makes me try. what keeps me awake. what I feel I'm guilty of. what I feel is wrong. every shade. from various distances. unveiled. possessing it. belonging to it. no longer feeling ashamed.

41

She's lowering her chin and lifting her shoulders. folding her arms and squeezing them together. what she always does when she's cold. for a moment I want her to dream of us being in the same place. years from now. when everything has slowed. what surrounds us. what spills over us. what has resulted. what I feel I've earned. I want my ashes scattered there. something she's slept through. I'm never speaking to him again. I feel a surge of strength. she'll meet him after work in the train station. I have nothing to do today. we're indestructible. we could kill if so desired. they're building an army. they speak in code. they're watching me from the rooftops. is she one of them. is she trying to corrupt me. could I fulfill some purpose. I would. I'd be grateful to be given direction. this is forbidden. it's strange to look at everyday things. they're accomplices. they're taking pleasure in it. doesn't he know that he's being intrusive. even the thought. even to imagine it. I'm drowning. I call to them. they seem not to notice. they've planned this. water's rushing into my lungs. they finally drag me out. they're digging in my pockets. they've found my wallet. I'm in debt. I've been given life and done nothing with it. I've been loved and have only used this to take what I want. he forgot to shave this morning. everything glows to her with finality. the way it'll be remembered. they huddle around the collision in their raincoats. I wish he'd move so I could sit down. the children are fighting over something. like every night. what must be endured to appreciate the emptiness. I never resist this urge. it doesn't make a difference now. he wants me to leave. I hope he suffers. I hope it's perfect for him. she follows me with her eyes. we wait in the cold. she sees the moon surrounded by clouds. like bites taken out of it. she's lost one of her earrings. where was she. what was she doing. I ignore all their warnings. someone has to be a victim. we're right for each other again.

42

We're sitting on the steps watching someone else's children chase the pigeons. some drop. roll in the dust and are dragged away by their wrists. does she understand me. what's to be understood. he needs to be fed. to get out of bed at a certain time. to be bought new clothes. his privacy. his thoughts. he often walks off then turns to view her from afar. imagines he's first laying eyes on her. assessing her beauty. she's always surprised by his little bursts of impatience. he's dishonest with himself. I pretend to be afraid. he's slow to react. she's led away. I'll be stranded. I'm trying to read their lips. the expressions on their faces. I hate doing this. that's what she needs to understand. it doesn't give me pleasure. but why does he. it's a sickness. it's bottomless. it's always hungry. I don't need to have faith in him. he'd continue on without me. valuable seconds are being wasted. she's spared. at last she can breathe deeply. I feel as though my laws should supersede theirs. that I'm better suited to keep her from harm. I wish it were earlier. I wish I lived closer. I wish we never had to work again. it now sounds strange to me. something he's fallen out of love with. it doesn't matter what they say. what they promise. it falls short of me. what'll I look to now. is this how death begins. one by one things losing their meaning. will it shift to something else. what I've yet to uncover. or is it progress. something I'm finished with. something I can discard like an empty container. why do I feel welcome here. no thought was given to me. everything I see and touch is theirs. what I bump into. what I swerve to avoid. no one needs me. no one cares if what I say is true. we're light as feathers. we've reached our full potential. our legs dangle uselessly. she puts up her hands to protect herself. forgetting we're no longer threatened. what she feared he was becoming. what she saw at times. we're absolved. we're incapable of thought.

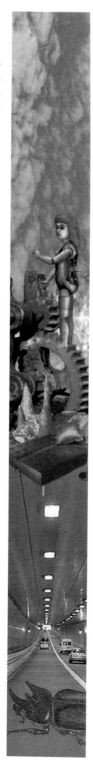

I was cursed. I met her. both of us were cursed. it'll never get better. every joint aches. all he sees displeases him. I've never tried. I've never wanted anything badly. it doesn't matter now. she's changed her mind. she isn't coming. finally I see her face approaching with all the others. there were droplets of joy in my fear. this should be enough. I want to walk past her. I want to follow them wherever they're going. around a corner that frees them from consequence. down a flight of stairs that holds them unaccountable. she's worried about something. I'm already seeing it resolved. forgotten. carried off piece by piece. I hope to hasten our inevitable ruin. I want the night to end in disaster. where did she come from. isn't she expected there. who did she mistake me for. a look returns mine. a pause is awaiting a reply. I should've been given a seat of honor. not tucked back here out of view. were they afraid of what I might do. a scream is caught in my throat. I stamp my feet softly. unimportantly. some are crying tears of joy. I thought their happiness would never fade. a purity I haven't known. I'm welcomed. she puts on this face. we haven't seen him in weeks. just hear him coming in. locking himself inside. I watch the rain land on the window and wonder what should be said. I don't share their sadness. like I've never shared their joy. she says nothing. it was a mistake to come here. I should abandon hope. I should assume the worst and try to move forward. their pity isn't necessary. I'm perfectly calm. I'm considering what I'm willing to sacrifice. what's really important. what's clutter. I'm clinging to every quiet moment. I'm trying to gather them in my arms. I'll let her sleep. I'll be almost perfectly still. it seems everyone is. then the train passes. then it returns to this. today will be busy. I'm already behind. what she keeps separate from me. what it seems she's nurturing. what I must get beyond. what isn't going away.

I can think whatever I want. strange I never realized this until very recently. I would go though the day censoring my thoughts. cutting things off before they'd become what I'd thought was forbidden. reproaching myself for allowing certain thought processes even to begin. gathering myself. what I should be thinking at this time. with this task at a hand. but it makes no difference. nothing is ever asked of me that requires a great deal of thought. that demands concentration. this is my reward for lacking ambition. this is a luxury I've earned. what I've unknowingly always pushed myself toward. it has no meaning. it'll never be judged. or heard. or assessed. there'll be temporary obstacles. noise. questions. but they can be dealt with. if I sound foolish. if I'm willing to. if I'm able to get over this fear. how does it look. what do they think of me. was what I said intelligible. I'll never know. yet everything's been targeted toward this. every minor decision. what I've been frightened into wanting. exactly where I'd have put a stop to it before. there are no laws here. it's kept inside. I take what I want. I can squeeze the life out of it. I don't need to explain myself to her. is this a danger. will it gain momentum. will it want out. am I strong enough to restrain it. I must be. the streets are safe. no one ever lays a finger on me. no one tries to rip what's clearly mine from my hands. have they always known this. will they ever know this. wherever I find myself. wherever my lack of foresight leads me. but there are those who can't. I've lived in such places. it gathers in the corners. it must run through them like a pack of wild dogs. and nothing to stop it. it was never seen as valuable. useful. necessary. dignified. but others misuse it. allow it too much influence. it misleads them. eats away at their insides. somewhere in between we sit down to breakfast. I'll change. I'll snip the last remaining string.

45

How do they compensate for this. what do they use to cover the holes. they won't hurt me. it's reinforced. it's seen as healthy. we're moving in a direction that's beneficial to us all. it'll make its way there. one day. eventually. it'll tame them. everyone will become harmless. she sees flaws in this. I'd meant for her to. I test it out. there's a woman with her back to me. she's always here at this time. strange these things should coincide. which'll last longer. what I need to respect if I want our happiness to grow. a crumb an ant is carrying up a hill. it's the first time I've walked in this direction down this street and haven't quickened my pace. now it's different. the buildings have been torn down and rebuilt while I was away. they look exactly the same. but I sense a change. everything looks more inviting. I'm visible. I'm worthy of acknowledgment. of the realization that we are the only two on the street. of what's beyond these doors. and how it can only be a dream. but it has a right to be. my hand reaches for the doorknob. it's freezing cold in my palm. I have money. where did it come from. where did we meet. it never mattered here. which would be most comfortable. what'll we talk about. we must talk at least a little. but it's better like this. not knowing anything. not being expected anywhere. dropping our things on the floor. this is wrong. what I must stop seeing freedom as. it's the opposite. nothing more insistently holds me where I am. she should be part of it. she should leave everything behind. just leave it burning. glowing. singing. bubbling. everything I say from now on will be sincere. when I hold her it won't be because I feel I should. and time will move backwards. every day we'll be the same age. what we've seen millions of times will always look new. will always fascinate her. she'll want to press it to her cheek. what we spend will find its way back to us. will slip beneath the door while we're crawling into bed.

46

Again I'm seeing us as bodies. again I'm wrong. we'll float from one to the next. fly. hop. swim. blow in the breeze. we'll be this color. have this taste. this smell. know all we need to. I'm seeing the flowers that were outside our door. we're walking into the water. it's up to our ankles. how the sunlight reflects off the surface of it. a path we've followed toads down. and seeing a bird who'd lost the others or wanted to be alone. I have happy memories of him. I think of jokes we've shared and I smile. it turns to sadness. what have I done for him to let this drift away. can I separate them. can I prevent what always follows. should I try to forget him completely. I can't. too much remains. he has claimed certain words as his own. words I need to use. years of my life. she gives me encouragement. she's made a difference. I consume this. the pain is slightly dulled. I need to rest. she feels cheated. men should be more resourceful. he's still motionless. blowing out the same candles and making the same wish. she leans forward. her face passes from shade into sunlight. something begins. she's undergone a transformation. they coddle this. all they've recently attained. I'm already mourning its loss. imagine it missing pieces. us returning to our usual routines. filling and emptying the wastebaskets. pacing back and forth. it's a shame the hours can only elapse one before the next. if only it were possible to multiply the monotony and consume it with one forced swallow. should I straighten up the room. something that has a beginning and an end. if I do it now I'll have nothing to do later. it's a worse feeling. nothing speaks. nothing symbolizes anything. they sit perfectly still and stare at me. they never change. even after a long absence. they're stubborn. it amazes me. why should it. why don't I believe something that's been proven to be true. countless times a day. as far as my comprehension can extend.

47

How did she get that bruise. it's too early. I'll accept anything she says. they've dropped whatever it was. they were only pretending. those books are full of empty pages. there's nothing in those bags. they leave and roam the streets all day. they jostle me every time I step outside. now they're listening at the door. it's part laziness. it's part a belief that I could be content with less. it's dishonesty. it's the chaos she'll inherit. each day they come. each day to their allotted corners. faces expressionless. hours between utterances. it's not this either. nor intimacy. nor flight. nor the destruction of walls. there'll still need to be secrets kept from us. even there. even after we've been purified. she's watching him. he yawns. rubs his eyes. looks around self-consciously. falls back into a trance. that's what I need. I've been forced into this. these are lies I've believed. where are they leading me. he believes lies too. it still takes effort. it still worries me. the last one was much closer. it's finding its way here. I'm afraid. I'm waiting. next it'll be something I can't afford to lose. I check underneath the bed and in the closet before turning off the lights. I press two fingers to the pulse in my neck. what was it. I was here alone and suddenly felt that all had been for naught. the great distance between us. no footprints. unspoiled. when it's at its worst. when what we usually blame is away. is off enjoying itself. where their joy makes sense. where their laughter is welcome. they can break things. they can hit each other. I didn't do it on purpose. I'm almost certain. if I can trust this. what comes if it's sought for. its persistence. I've never done anything on purpose. still it's with us. when she speaks it dies. I flick its little insectlike remains off my forearm. what can she teach me. how does it feel. is it touchable. is it still years from now. I'm not tired but I lay down. I'm not cold but I wrap a blanket around me. all the usual sounds.

48

Is it an accusation. something I'd never condemn him for. is it a way to look from the outside at something universally condemned. she apologizes yet again. she keeps her visits short. for me to say anything would make matters worse. immediately afterward I wash away the blood and sleep like a child. the temptation is stronger than usual today. now that there's no one to scold me. my voice has changed. I've plucked out the eyes I'd used to look into hers. she's exactly the same as she's always been. only now she's gone. I feel at ease to deteriorate. to be true to my former self. I'm planning an act of cowardice I know I'll be too cowardly to commit. I keep the lights dim. it's like talking to a shadow. goes out after dark. looks up and down the street. walks around the block. continues waiting. I need to convince someone else of this. that it's not without its dignity. is meant to pacify. is necessary for our survival. she moves slowly. with sadness. picking things up and putting them down. the clinks on the porcelain sink. turning on the water. we've lost. we've been dreading this morning. all yesterday we were afraid to move. we were afraid to lose track of time. we've never accepted it. this isn't ours. it isn't anyone's. we're getting closer. we hardly complain. it'll end. it's in the way we move our bodies. our subtle defiance. empty gestures. how we keep out of each other's way. where it drops him. sometimes I look. I wonder if I have anything to do with it. what he can't find here. why it takes so much effort. will it get worse. it's here. it's mine. has he ever tried. it doesn't do any good. who'll go first. I'm in the middle. why does he need me. we hear a pin drop. I'm nervous. she's disappointed. I'll spring to life at the wrong time. a color carries itself in softly. it'll wait for me. it'll think I'm no good. she's the opposite of me. she's giving. if I hold her tightly it'll strengthen this. it'll shut out our everyday needs.

49

He looks sick. this isn't enough. we aren't enough. they're through with me. I'm ashamed to be seen. I've never doubted it. I feel worry more intensely than I've ever felt anything. it isn't her. no one even knows who she is. he's alarmed when he realizes how little he means to the world. it's my duty. all that's ever asked of me. the only thing I can do. my function. she's never felt this. gets dressed and goes off without complaining. he lingers. don't look at my imperfections. my mistakes. there's no record being kept. no one knows these things about me. it's soothing. I'm weightless. music drifts across the hall. he keeps me warm. someone sifts through a garbage can. someone else makes us laugh. nothing is a matter of life or death. nothing warrants such seriousness. he's ours. he's something to trust. she wants to escape this. her eyes drift off to the side. does she picture herself there alone. I spoke to him only once. he muttered something. I hurt her once. then it became easy. it's in my heart. I'm not even thinking of it then suddenly it's there. will I ever be forgiven. does anyone need my forgiveness. everyone else has forgotten everything. I blame where I'm from. I blame anyone who's ever spent time with me. an imbalance of this. a tiny spark. everything moving much too quickly. she sits in silence. applies a fresh layer. expects a thunderous collision. we flutter in perfect harmony. we never need to speak. he makes an adjustment. nothing effects him. from my room I see the train station and the newsstand. people are flipping through magazines. he isn't the answer. he doesn't have any answers. but I'm cradling him in my arms. I'm doting on him as if he were helpless. nothing I wish for will ever come true. that's what this feeling is. failure works its way into everything. what was treasured. what was longed for. I saw its bones finally poke through. I want to rush there. I want to adapt to it. learn to speak. to begin our recovery.

He partially opens his eyes. hundreds of pairs of feet in seconds. I'm a mouse scurrying from hole to hole. happy with what is unwanted. will I survive. will I hear her voice again. has she forgotten me. I'll curl up here. he looks like he's taken a kick to the stomach. I check that the door's locked. my morning's ruined. it's dim. nothing gets through. I'm lazily at peace under a thin layer of sweat. he's being stubborn. there's a trail of water from the bathroom to where she's sitting near the window. she's wearing a bathrobe. she's thinking it isn't worth it. surrender is in his voice and eyes. or when he's only breathing. it's too deep. I'll never reach it. I'll never be able to hold it up and poke at it to prove to him that it's harmless. I've learned never to ask him what he wants for himself. what he hopes the future might bring. I wasn't trying to upset him. to pick this apart. I'd just like to hear him talk about it. to know what the days are moving toward. most people's lives are easy. even if it appears they aren't. they're happy with what they have. they must be. they continue. will it come to me. will I grow smaller until it fits perfectly. I sense it. she's going to provoke me. I wish she had a prettier smile. they're lost. they're hollow. at least I've resisted. at least I'm still recognizable. I want him to question this. I want it to nest inside him. no one ever admits they're wrong about something that big. about everything they've ever believed. not to others. not to themselves. someone'll have to lose. something'll have to be resolved. some wanted the obvious. or never knew better. or were lonely. or needed something to talk about. some had integrity but changed. is she being too harsh. why shouldn't she. it's a simple pleasure. it's an achievement. she starts again. I don't give my own emotions such dignity. it wasn't for fear or love. or some concrete vision. I knew what ate at me. I knew what made me feel powerless.

I pulled things out and they grew in again. I knew what they saw me as. I sat with him and we stopped caring. we knew we'd be rescued. we didn't want to be. if we're disguised. if we're playing dead. it continues onto the next. it never tires. it never draws attention to itself. I'm resolved to this. what's solid. boredom and amusement. what's within hope. I don't envy her for still believing in other possibilities. it was a long time before he noticed her intelligence. now he resents it. her ability to pinpoint the flaws in his reasoning. to want further explanation where he'd been purposely vague. I have no past. I was born this way. everything will pour out and harden. cause us to stick. what occurs to me now. things I've never been told. what I've let lie to spare her feelings. I want to see it. we're all fools. I want to know where she hides this. there are crawl spaces. there's just enough darkness to cover her movements. still I'm surprised by her lack of caution. something I'm intended to see. I leave. I wanted to be alone. I am. I wanted time. I have entire days at my disposal. I eat as fast as I can. I return to my desk and just sit here. even if I succeed. even if I'm able to. it won't bring to me what I'd hoped it would. they'll draw still further away. effort wasted. months wasted. her patience won't last forever. it won't be taken as an insult. it won't be a ringing alarm. he won't make time for it. there are many just like this. what people resort to when they're less capable. tossed somewhere with contempt. I avoid even the smallest exchanges. simple pleasantries. what's expected. what's the most I can hope for. what's the least. it isn't a sacrifice. it's selfish. it'll cause even greater confusion. we're not brothers. we're not equals. one wants acceptance. that's over for me. it's been made impossible. am I regretting it. is it doing damage. I count them. everything's wrong. insurmountable. I need kind words from him. I need someone to teach me.

He was taken. it's not real. even though it's been explained to me. it moves forward. later it seems something salvaged from a shipwreck. something strangely familiar. has he had these feelings. he couldn't have. not ever. not even before he understood how things worked. he was senseless. I remember when I first arrived. I was overjoyed. every step I took. I was hungry but I wanted to keep walking. he's casting this aside. he's noticing how late it's become. I'm on the verge of another bad decision. it was awkward. it clung to me. it changed how she felt. this silence is spiteful. I see a warning. a sleepless watery look of disbelief. beyond this line I feel taken advantage of. shivering in the cold. it lasts days. I was two years younger. we're full of them. what I said. now I sweep the dead leaves aside. he'll speak and it'll be broken. it isn't a life. it isn't a memory. it could be easy. the light I've shone on her could be extinguished. I could be shaken empty. I'm the exact color of the wall. I'm the exact sound of the wind through a window mistakenly left open. I don't want pity. I pity her. I don't want to be warm. or to sleep. or to keep giving to what always wants more. still these healthy glows. I wave up to him in a second story window. he's never succumbed to this. her feet were throbbing so I carried her. what does he think I do all day. how do all these people fill all this time. what does she do. can she sense my eagerness. the desire to trail humbly behind her beauty. I compare them. this is what I curtail to. both equally. unhappily. it calms. it can't be heard. she walks out. I don't know who she becomes. this is my responsibility. I felt differently then. it sparkles in the light of what was lost. if she'd obeyed me. if she'd stayed. I'd like to see where she lives. if it's as lonely as she says. the things that have accumulated. what she's saved. don't answer her. stop coming here. it could never have gone beyond this. even before we spoke.

53

They're falling off. it's softer than I ever imagined. it's small. it's flawless. somehow they don't notice us. I don't want to move forward. this is enough. it's the only way I can comprehend it. we are invisible. she's reading my thoughts. she's always known. it's real. they're different. they're frightening. why I've learned to protect myself. what happens here. myself and them. we shouldn't spoil our appetites. they grow like flowers. I've never met her. I agree completely with both. it doesn't stop. but it already has. I'm hanging by my ankles. I'm too easily distracted. she runs out to greet me. I tell her how I've been spending my time. I don't leave anything out. I'm straining my eyes. does this explain it. they're under a spell. no remorse. no second thoughts. it's going to happen again. nothing she could do would change this. I've seen where it's hidden. she's in denial. he should've come sooner. I don't accept his excuses. kneel. be an animal. give me total control. I'll cure them. I'll rid them of pettiness. prejudice. they were willing. they enjoyed it. lost themselves. I knew him. I could see him from my window. out in the open. I need to smell that scent again. I need to be eaten. I lived there. I was loved there. I was relieved of my burden. before I came she didn't exist. she was trapped in birth. why did he tell her. why did he steal her. she's my link to everything I've never understood. she refuses to accept this. what I'd choose as our paradise. I want everyone else dragged off. I want them set free. told never to return. forced to begin again with nothing. we'll sleep here tonight. she's making it our home. the sun's setting. no one else can see it. they're doing what children do when they've run off. I run in and out of doors. I bring back things I think she'll like. things I like. things that will sustain us. until there are no more possibilities. until I've learned everything. what'll be left of her. I'll quietly slip out the door.

Her picture's facing me. it's like we're alone. she doesn't need to move. I don't need to pretend I've never done this before. all of them have this weakness. all of them cave in when faced with it. we're waiting for the train again. we're cold. it's noisy. they're curious about us. they look each time she touches me. they aren't real. they're stories told to calm frightened children. we're standing in line behind them. he's been listening. we gather our things up. find a place to sit. he tapped on the glass. wanted someone to chase him. they seem neither happy nor sad. just people in the middle of their morning routines. how various. how unrelated. yesterday was bad. especially the afternoon. I got carried away. doubt filled my heart. it was like dying. I watched time tick by. I was angry. do something. anything. act as if I'm here. perhaps it heightens one's sense of hearing. I want to sound sincere. I want to be sincere when I say it. I want to lower myself until it's true. I need rest. I fear his disapproval. I created her. all of them. where they came from. where they'd like to be. how many teeth are missing. I'm under glass. someone's recording how often I toy with this. I wait for him in the miserable evening. I've let him convince me it's a form of respect. I push myself. it's my reward. it's the only thing he says that I can relate to. she's so close to me. our necks are almost wrapped around each other's. she's sucking the foolish daydreams straight from my skull. did she have a good time. have I given them reasonably happy lives. he doesn't want me involved. it's too dark to read. my ears are ringing. my limbs are numb. abandon me. three weeks pass. I swear on my life. on this dead weight. on all that has slid through my hands. she'd have no use for me. I'd be in the way. she doesn't like her new job. always on her feet. she doesn't want to go back. I want to change my face and body each day to keep his attention. I never want to grow old. a matter of time.

I snuck up behind her. the smallest glimmer of hope gives rise to fantasies dumbfounding in their clarity. no matter how long I sleep I still wake grudgingly. they're numbed by the sunlight. they're unsuspecting. I turned in her direction. I'd meant to kiss her forehead. something innocent and unthreatening in the light that so annoyed me. as peaceful as a fishbowl. I take a few steps. I give off a weak reflection. everything fades. I've been followed. my neck is stiff. my fingernails are dirty. my spirit is crushed. I drift downward until we're cheek to cheek. until she absorbs my stupidity. our jugular veins intertwine and beat twice as loudly. there was something in him I was never able to bend. I'm grateful it ended when it did. he's alone tonight. no one's there to comfort him. he never stops twisting. stumbles upon her escape tunnel. dug with a spoon every night while he was sleeping. she must be exhausted. I need to know if it's him. something that invites me. something that could turn on me. that's sick. that's brave. it couldn't be anyone else. I don't want her to come back yet. this isn't a real day. it doesn't have the dignity. the potential. I'm outside of it. I want to be included. then it passes. I'm happy I'm here. what can we talk about. reasons to worry. ways to determine how little sympathy I'm capable of. it comes with time. humiliation. cruelty. if we're to be in awe of wisdom. kindness. please don't come. please stay away until I feel I've done enough. I'm proud to have been rejected by them. it rains down on me. he sits down. she stares at his face. watches him yawn. frown. she's determined. it's stronger than reason. it's stronger than our love. these are her feet. these are her shoulders. I'm rescued. I can wake. I can want to communicate. he's at the center. he resents me being secretive. I love her because we fear the same things. because we've made up our minds. I can blame her. I can brick her in with this.

56

I'd like for him to say what's on his mind. speak until he collapses. or anyone. just to prove to me that they have thoughts. hearts. I had high hopes for him. he could bear anything. he never talked about his personal life. his desk was always neat. I've only ever seen the aftermath. brushing up against me in crowded places. adding to the tension. it's so easy. I'm surprised. I thought at the last moment I'd freeze. that something would emerge from the chaos and assume its proper place. a forgotten detail. a nearly forgotten voice. a remnant from a promise made. but there was nothing. silence. an awareness of the onlookers. at last a cleansing peace. they'll no longer have to walk around me. it wasn't misery. or disgust. or a sense of unfairness. just feeling ineffective. landing harmlessly. she thinks I don't worry about her. every movement. no matter how slight. dissatisfaction. I imagine them swarming around me. dozens of bodies pressed tightly together underneath this blinding light. those doomed to constantly wander. those who don't attempt to understand. those being suspiciously affectionate. she and I are powerless. we know nothing. our worst fears. I need to stop. I need to think. he doesn't look entirely unhappy. has he changed. is it an awkward dance. laughing he swings open the door. I can be violent. I can take every weakness in mankind and bring it straight down on her neck. I can knock out his teeth. they're giggling because they're nervous. it makes it easier for her. I wanted her as my own. I tried so hard. what I thought she'd want to hear. kill this time together. feel out of place together. miss things. I've learned. it's laughable. it's hopeless. it's a form of worship not to trust her. it overpowers me. it makes my decisions. it stirs me. it dresses me. it tells me when to eat. she walks into the room with timid little steps as if interrupting a brain surgery. I don't belong here. I don't belong anywhere.

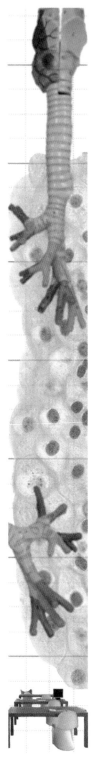

I saw her this morning. she looks content. a spoiled pet. no need to look elsewhere. any noise unnerves me. puts me on guard. a place we went together. entering. rubbing our hands. enjoying the warmth. I want her attention. I've built this for her. if not for me we'd be sinking. frost would be forming on us. there was plenty of time to place everything safely out of view. I'll always be overheard. I'll always be under suspicion. she'll think the worst. her narrow view of what's healthy. I try to grasp it. I try to make it work for me. she's a prison. parts of me go in and never return. I try to remember. I try to stand in the right place. make a living. be thankful. if I try hard it'll be good. where is this stated. what assurance do I have. what'll be my response. I won't answer. this room follows me everywhere. I'm waiting for this to dry. I'm waiting for the activity to die down. curiosity is killing her. why won't he come. does he think it'd be a bother. he knows I don't have anything else to do. I make up faces. I make up people. painful looking. uncertain. no purpose. not wanting to continue. what else is there. she sits down. butterflies in her stomach. I don't want to be disturbed. he's still hurting. a delayed response from the last time he saw her. it was such a joy. what's happened. pointing a finger. senses her delight. I don't feel it. I lay there and don't feel a thing. I let it grow. I wait for someone to come and stop me. I don't care. it takes too much concentration. the first emotion I remember. then always. then every single day. I'll survive. I'll use then what I'm letting go to waste now. it could easily happen again. I don't know what caused it. or how to prevent it. I'll never be able to win their respect. this is my lowest moment. I hang my head. within myself I feel my dreams and hopes forced to submit to this safety. this numbing consistency. I've given up. it's such a relief. it washes over me. a cause for celebration.

58

I'm pretending. these are lies. I've never felt superior. I want to be lowered even further in their eyes. I want to band them closer together. I want them to be unified. nameless. identical. a mass of eyeballs and waving tongues. I want for it to require courage for any one of them to associate with me. I'll have no defense. they won't understand individually. only together. to rely on each other for acceptance and direction. from where I'm perched I can see the dangling nerves. I'm looking for certain characteristics. who's holding hands. who's beyond corruption. which share a resemblance. I can't begin. I can't stop looking out the window. hopefully I'll be more productive when the sun goes down. it's hard to keep a secret. it drains all my energy. I never thought she'd resort to this. I shouldn't have been so honest. he asked about the future and I almost laughed in his face. my real self. I'll never make much sense to him. he protects her. she hopes to be dragged to the surface and revived. will I turn or will I go straight and continue walking home. I still don't know. I've already pivoted and am heading toward a mirage. the day is over. no one'll see me. he's in one corner. she's in another. I hope she doesn't resist. she needs new things. they glisten and yelp. should this require strength. he thinks he can wait forever. I was too impatient. she loved it. she enjoyed every minute. she's distorted things. if I step forward. if I force myself to exert my will. everything changes. everything comes to me. I can trace it back years. there were different paths I should've taken. every time I make a promise I feel part of myself die. they're crushed. they never even make it out of their shells. a small hole where they'd tried. indistinguishable from the rest of this mess. tiny shards stuck to boots. in the crevices of tire treads. what they'd possessed was better than wisdom. better than unlimited riches.

I watch helpless as they grow smaller and stop existing. I can't hear them but I'm sure they're there. laughing. something of little consequence. something that has nothing to do with me. or them. I've made myself sick to experience the joys of recovery. to watch hour by hour the color return. I encouraged her. I encourage any form of idiocy. they identify with me. they adore me. they discover it through various channels. their ugliness. I'm responsible. I oversaw its assembly. in a way it's proof of her kindness. I'm ashamed of how much time I have on my hands. it'd drive him crazy. she asked for this. it sat too long and lost its purpose. if I had influence. if what I said became law. she and I aren't the only ones sprawled out on the grass allowing the sunlight to penetrate our closed eyelids. turning the darkness red. there's a gentle breeze. children are chasing something. I bury my face in her. she's ticklish. all she's ever seen is beauty. this misfortune. this deficiency. losing something irreplaceable. what does it remind me of. no one'll care. she's full of life. not afraid to be seen. genuinely happy. listens with growing discomfort as I explain. who meets on these corners. clutters these stairways. sharing with each other their blurry fragments of sky blue pasts. it's more honest than the truth. I've rested too long here. I hadn't been expecting her. I can smell him through the wall. I can taste what he's eating. no one will enter. I lock the door and rattle it in its hinges to assure her. I can't move without knocking something over. she can't stay long. their playfulness makes him lonely. it's new to us. being together but being unhappy. does he care. I show him where it hurts. I should ask her. I should listen. I'm a very small part of this. I'm almost useless but they still find things for me to do. it begins and I know I'll survive. then I'm not sure. I can't think straight. it's nothing. I lie down in it.

What I know they'll never find a use for. what I wake thinking of. going to places where I'm recognized. there's nothing more to him. she'll stay here for a while. eventually she'll leave. he tells me he's happy. moves closer. she hadn't understood him. still I feel he should be punished. torn down. she won't tell him. she doesn't want him to feel pressured. it's a perfect mixture of contentment and boredom. she turns and looks at him one last time from the bottom of the stairs. a hand waves sadly back to her. she's the only one on the train. he looks exhausted. he'll never wake up on time. I got home and found her note. read it once. fell deeply asleep. it's when they're all here together that I feel the strongest urge to disrupt their peace of mind. it'd only take seconds. I clench my teeth. close my eyes as tightly as I can. the urge passes. someday it'll overpower me. nothing'll ever be the same. she positions herself carefully and waits for his response. it just seems as though it should take more time and effort. I stand a safe distance away and try to eavesdrop. he drifts off. he falls apart. just when we needed him. just when he could've shown that he appreciates all we've done. she'll sacrifice. she'll let some things slide. these next few days will be intolerable. there's little I can do to dull the effects. the blood will pound through her veins while they all wait in silence. I never turn my head fast enough to catch them in the act. this level of contempt excites them. this selfishness. this disregard. the strange nature of their friendship. all other aspects of their lives must pale by comparison. we've designated a new place to meet. I'll always be early. hours unaccounted for. it surrounds me. it makes my knees weak. I hurry home and lock the door. I want to finish. I want a reason to doubt myself. to wonder if it leads to other things. I have to do it now. later I won't have the chance. I'll know better then. I'll need more.

She's deep in thought. I'm not even here. the times when she becomes another person. the room's empty. the world's uninhabited. I want to live longer. he falls and splits his head open. the crowd keeps moving. a rolling wave of concentration. of having somewhere to be. I beg for privacy. his blood soaks into the knees of my pants. am I seeing this clearly. she sits on the corner of the bed. a soft breeze blows spitefully. she's done nothing to brighten up the place. I don't want any reminders that there's more to it than this. that it extends forever. that I'll never see all of it. everything combines to make her this way. the soft voices. the clock ticking. the color of the walls. the dust in the corners. it's just like a lullaby. sends me out into the fog. everyone's half asleep. his voice gives me goose bumps. he's torturing himself. I saw it flicker. diverted my eyes. dozens of lies were exposed as such. it doesn't bother him but I can no longer ignore it. I get nervous when she's silent. I worry somehow I've let her down. regardless of how angry she gets she'll always walk next to me. she'll always hold my hand. it eventually lessens. then it's my turn to be unhappy. what else do we have in common. I'm jealous of such innocence. she's lying down. she's turning toward the wall. she has a different idea of what's meaningful. less misshapen than mine. what's she doing wrong. what am I doing wrong. it's penetrated so deeply that it makes all attempts at intimacy unrecognizable. seem their opposite. met with suspicion. someone is always watching us. I owe him my life. he feels I'm not beyond hope. I don't hate her. I don't hate anyone. only what's taken root in them. what they have such faith in. my feet are aching. I look down all the narrow alleyways. my persistence will be rewarded. I hold the umbrella above her. my clothes are dripping. she'll never believe I'm anything other than a weakling. had already known then. was looking past me.

Why is this happening. I ask myself each time. I thought I'd been careful. it won't happen again. I'll ignore it until it overwhelms me. has enough time passed. could I try harder. I don't want her to see me like this. it's the only explanation I can give. what I won't admit to but still hope to be forgiven for. it's eating away at everything. my dreams. the acceptance I've earned. he thinks I'm avoiding him. I'm not. but I want him to feel hurt. it's late. he should be getting home. it isn't obvious. we won't have to talk about it. he's too sensitive. I doubt any of them are sincerely in love. he's needed there. he's turned his back on me. it's strong in him. I'm something hidden in the back of a drawer. until it's gone. until I'm told. I have time to myself. he causes me to wonder if all my longings aren't unhealthy. he leaves an imprint. why I hardly ever go to see him. I can almost see and hear what he describes. that my hands have touched the same things. that I've swallowed them. I practice telling lies while looking in the mirror. I practice being certain. this laziness worries her. what if someday she needs him. he leaves like a tooth pulled from its roots. all the time in the world. he borrowed money from me. he's enjoying himself. he trembles with impatience. I kissed her once. I've kept it a secret. the sun was coming up and it was cold. the wind blew sheets of newspaper around. someone was sweeping the train platform. it was the closest we'd ever come to asking anything of each other. if only each day could begin this soft and beautifully. seeing something being born. lying in bed wide awake. how we're similar. the same direction. the same determination. it's easy to imagine those my shoulders. those her stomach muscles. is she only pretending that I have the upper hand. if I loosen my grip will she tear out my eyes. I hold her away from me. my arms are longer than hers. she's still moving. a million little annoyances.

63

He agreed to go at once and attempt to revive her. now's my chance. I wish she were someone else. I wish he could provide for me. she always gets on the train at this stop. at this time. she's always with the same people. I try to listen to what they're saying. I won't mention my worries. it may be months before the circumstances change. to simply worry does nothing. I've earned the right to gluttony. some gratitude. they've increased their expectations. new routines must be developed. the wind blows the door shut. her looks are fading. I can speak to her without blushing. I've accomplished something. she notices it every time she talks to him. he's always the same. she doesn't help. she doesn't treat me any differently. my efforts are worthless. she was talking to me. I've led her here. sometimes things go according to plan. am I being a pest. I envision how it'd be if she'd allowed this to continue. if I'd survived. she looks back at him. he'll do anything to look busy. he picks things up. carries them a short distance. puts them down. from his knees he can see everything. clouds. stars. I have a feeling it'll soon be ending. he quickly springs to his feet. all of my struggles have been in vain. each time I grudgingly threw the covers aside. each time I ignored what I wanted. each attempt to be rational. each time I considered her feelings. it amounts to nothing. I should've scared hope away. sank peacefully into ruin. allowed everything to wither. I can't hide from him forever. it's a stream that flows through me. what needs to be done now. if I ever actually get what I want. the past. the reasons I have to be angry with him. but the need to keep my dignity. the belief that one shouldn't show anger. the usual sounds of someone returning home at the end of the day. I can see the top of his head through the window. I watch the doorknob turn. she'd say all of this was wrong. she'd dismiss it with a wave of her hand.

64

I'll be stronger then. it'll be concise. in a way I never thought of. only a few more blocks. slide the key in the lock and turn. they're so predictable. standing on corners as if waiting for someone. checking their watches. retreating rapidly as if suddenly remembering something. the thin layer between us. I'll disappear within. I realize what's happening. purity doesn't exist. lies protect us. I'm the last to know. the most susceptible. the least resourceful. quivering in my capsule. I look in her eyes and all I see is joy. she dances in his absence until she's too worn out to stand. something always survives. I find it if I look hard enough. if I believe that it'll be there. finally he enters the darkness and his privacy. let them eat each other alive. it must beat just like a heart. if both of them were plucked from this and isolated it'd be seen that they're exactly the same. who built these towers. who burrowed these tunnels. I can't be bothered to lift a finger. even pressed closely together the two of us would freeze. I only want comfort. I want to grow old. I want to rest. I want to forfeit every remaining opportunity. one day I'll finish. it'll stink of desperation. it'll be rushed. missing pieces. it'll collapse and bury its inhabitants. he'll arrive and ask what I've been doing. I'll point to the puddle of drool. he's disturbing me. the first sound he makes. the first footstep of his that I'm able to hear. then the thousands more that follow. if I block my eyes he'll touch me. if I hide behind a door I'll somehow taste that he's here. is she coming back soon. has she had enough time to recover. I can't handle any more disappointment. again I fall. I know she'll come out. I know she can't resist me when she thinks that I'm in need. he turns his back and she begins examining each one. the shapes and colors. I understand why they're so admired. why they've been raised up. why even the leeches that feed off them feel they deserve some of the praise.

65

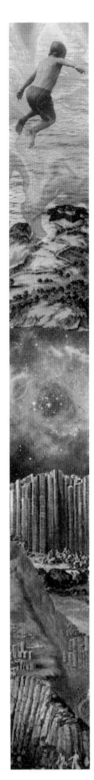

I want everyone to see me with him. I want them to know we understand each other. he was on his way to meet her. finally something would be resolved. I'm purposely disintegrating. renouncing my will. my individuality. this humility inflames his sense of martyrdom. makes him feel even more deserving. even more sincere. I'm doing what I feel is expected of me. eating when I'm not hungry. showing concern when I truly don't care. I disguise things for their sake. I can sleep standing straight up. I've overcome temptation. I've kept her whereabouts a secret. I've made her feel safe. she can make me happy. he never thinks of anything else. he pauses. he wishes he had something to say to her. he continues on his way. I've been sleeping well lately. I wake earlier than usual. he ties her to this. tightens the ropes around her wrists. was it unexpected. did her heart skip a beat. he's the only one that ever does anything to help. they'd let her starve. they'd let her leave without saying good-bye. she left because she was lonely. he no longer came. he'd found others. it seemed to her like he'd been kidnapped. kept in a room. brainwashed. learned to love and hate accordingly. never doubted that he belonged there. I'm not alone in this. there's strength in numbers. stumbles. steadies himself. points an accusing finger. she resents him. this has never ceased. infests everything. nothing is sacred. the enemy is anything that reflects the light too brightly. anything eager to distinguish itself. she says she doesn't care what he thinks. I don't believe her. he's never far from her thoughts. tries to act distant but I can see her frustration. looks lost to draw him nearer. is saddened by her own polite little laugh. why she tries so hard. how she still cares. I'd do anything to prove her wrong. to make her give in and deflate. it'll be gradual. I'll be patient. I'll notice small things. someday she'll agree with me. tell me everything. admit that I was right.

66

I hear things. I open doors and look in rooms I know are empty. I enjoy it. it makes me feel like a child. if something were there. if anything ever is. does this mean that I'm off the hook. do I still have to go to work. can't I follow it where it takes me. I want to laugh from there at what I once considered mine. she'd like to let him fade. grow lighter and lighter until his hum can't be heard. what happens when I'm not there. I'll never know. only what he says. I'm too trusting. too unobservant. glaring mistakes. it'll be months before I have a chance to redeem myself. I was tempted to destroy everything. effort and effort and never success. I'm still expected to smile while I'm here. to act as if I couldn't want more. I'll come home and she'll ask me how it was. we're repeating ourselves. we're becoming weaker. there's hope. she's certain. I wish he knew that it was me who caused him all this suffering. I won't allow them to be called narrow-minded. or to be blamed for my laziness. the majority of her time is spent waiting for him to apologize. she can't concentrate. everything hinges on this. everything else has been pushed aside. I wish we'd never met. he talks to himself when he thinks that no one else can hear. always the same things. each with their own little rituals. I remember this nervousness. she must've lied. she must be laughing. the tide must have swept her away. my face is unfamiliar to them. what's he doing here. how did he get in. it's dark and I'm already dreaming. I nearly collide with another. I'm a child again. I'm being carried to my bedroom. I'm always safe. am I paying attention. is there more to what she said. what she hasn't said. someone's been in my room. some of my things are missing. I'll stay up all night. I'll guard it with my life. I'll begin to sleep in the daytime instead. I have no influence over her. she comes and goes as she pleases. I thought I'd made it clear. who's on her side. where does she get these ideas.

How often does she find herself here. does it lessen its value. I don't want a direct answer. do I have a right to intervene. I try to make as little noise as possible. he's careless. caresses a patch of stubble just below his lip that he missed while shaving. perhaps he'd meant to provoke her. she thought of him this morning as she stood before the mirror. he's completely detached. neither happy nor sad. doesn't even get angry at me anymore. I'm on the verge of great happiness. no one asks me to explain. as if all of them would've done exactly the same. out of the corner of his eye he watches her put her coat on. should he go with her. she wonders if she saw her. if he'll come. I'm finally able to predict my own behavior. recognize in advance situations in which I'll be powerless to act otherwise. she wants to live by the sea. shows me a dot on a map. I'm stealing her from another. she still considers his feelings. it's a habit. I've sensed it dissolving. she's waiting to be released. she's sacrificing something. she never misses an opportunity to mention his name. I've persisted. I'm always here. I answer all her questions. I swallow. I can't taste it. I want to stay alive. I want to quit my job. I never want to see any of those people again. she thought he'd left months ago then she saw him one evening. it was dark. I couldn't see his face but instantly recognized his voice. he'd left and returned. moved back into his old place. I'm sitting next to her. I didn't know then. he stands before us. she'd defied him. it's consistent. the crows always rip open the garbage bags and let the trash blow up and down the street. I'm finished for the day. it's dark. I'm unwinding. across the street I can see into the window of the ballet school. it's the only light on. I can see them from their waists up. I can see their feet as they raise their legs. I'll only ever know them as this. they never suffer. they never need to be fed. I've never done anything gracefully.

I've never wanted to make progress. I've always felt that any movement forward was costly. any achievement or obstacle overcome was the death of something beautiful. innocent and irretrievable. I wanted everything to stay the same. he's watching things deteriorate or bloom. I'll live solely to avoid such emptiness. I attacked him. I was glad there were so many people around or I'd have never had the nerve. she thought it was a cockroach on the wall. threw a book at it. it didn't move. they've forgotten about us. we're dying of thirst. they resent that I'm here. where do I put my eyes. this was a mistake. I should've gone home hours ago. it's freezing outside. it's a long walk. I'll get sick again. she tries to convey everything at once. when it's bad. when it gets worse. I want her to be specific. I want one concrete example. she only moves closer. presses herself against me. I must draw my own conclusions. little hands that look like a child's in mine. I can blow tiny pieces of her pain away. he loved me last week. now he doesn't answer. what distinguishes today from yesterday. it adds up. its effects are only noticeable after years and years. all I have to show for this is our fragile friendship. I'd tell him I think its destiny but I know it'd make him think less of me. I insult him instead. I'll grow another heart. she clings to what makes her weak. will always need something to blame. he can listen until he knows everything. until I'm only bones. she doesn't dare turn her head. he finally realizes where he is. admires the sense of ceremony. the gloomy backdrop. is it foolishness or strength to never admit defeat. she's dropped off the face of the earth. she must be happier. I could hide from him but I feel that this is my duty. the price I must pay for my relative freedom. a debt I owe my past. when his anger softens he returns to reaffirm his beliefs. each time we say less and less. regretfully replace unused weapons. wish each other well. go separate ways.

69

I'm the worst of them. from whom they expect the least. I'm the least honest. the weakest and slowest. the cause of this terrible silence. it's all my fault. this room. how cold it gets. the disappointment I see in everyone I come across. the broken mirror. the holes in things. what I do for a living. his failure. how he never moves. his declining health. how it grays and falls apart. how they're growing into it. I can survive on even less. he's making excuses. no one could be content with this. I did the best I could. I see now why they worry. what he ran away from. what drove her to another. the days of tiptoeing back and forth between attempts to understand. no one can connect me to this. he isn't making sense. those that knew better. those that knew what to expect drifted out past yelling distance. out past the furthest iceberg. she's immune to misfortune here. the ground won't shake. poisonous gas won't seep beneath the door. no one will ever find her. they can give up on me. he can treat me any way he likes. at least he's someone different. she's the most loving. he's the most levelheaded. she's the most unique and spirited. I'm embarrassed when I think about it. how I lavished praise and almost confided in her. she doesn't realize that to me it isn't a sacrifice. that I'd otherwise be bored to tears. we feel the sun on our cheekbones and shoulders. this is how easily I hang my head. how I hope something will carry me off. I wanted to savor every second. flatten them in between my palms and spread them out before me. all that had been kept from me. what's hidden behind their backs. what's slid into secret compartments just before I enter the room. now dangles from the ceiling. swarms up me from the floor. I'm able to succeed at what it felt absurd to dream. her frown doesn't mean anything. is no longer a cause for alarm. only that she's lost in thought. we heard a loud noise and she gripped me tighter. we swerved to avoid an outstretched hand.

I can feel her spine through her shirt. it's the same as it was. it wasn't one of my creations. they're crouching behind garbage cans. they're dressed like butterflies. waiting to pounce. or to fly. I cough loudly so as not to take them by surprise. she's worried that we've made a wrong turn. that safety and warmth'll elude us all night. the first time she's ever had to trust me. just a little further. through a gate. it'll extend forever. in any direction we choose. happy births. slow peaceful deaths. and beyond. corners where shadows never gather. where eyes don't peek out from nests. this drop'll expand. it'll grow and learn to walk. it'll look down on us as we die. she climbs the walls with the grace and dexterity of a spider. her fingers are tensed. straightened. I need this. what I'll be able to close my eyes and see afterward. what I'll keep alive within me. nothing's left. it's done and expected again. a constant hum sounds just below what we can hear. I'll check to be certain. I woke up in the middle of the night. my throat burned. I noticed the door slightly ajar. my breath fogs the window. she nudges me aside. I wish she only laughed at my jokes. I wish we were the only two in the world. but there's him. a mouse that popped its head out of a hole. less than a week has elapsed. I sit alone and think of all the things I'd like to say to her. all the beauty of simple solutions. all the time wasted. he paces around his desk. puts on a sweater but still feels cold. it happened so suddenly. a few hours ago I went out without a jacket. she stayed in bed this morning. it may be my fault for keeping her out late. should I feel responsible. but I never insisted. I didn't bind her. he thinks I don't remember his name. I never want to startle him. I suspect he can float and walk through walls. he crosses my mind at these moments. these things are closer to his heart. perhaps he's more entitled to them. he doesn't allow himself to look. she's a threat to everything. to all of us.

She doesn't have any privacy. I consider her a statue. it's best not to speak to her. to believe that she was given a tiny little heart. she was right to call these lies. why is my stomach rumbling. why am I sleepy. she came back and he returned to normal. we have nothing in common. I'm beyond such foolishness. I'd never try so desperately. I feel it taking away pieces of my soul. a newly formed addiction. afterward I don't remember anything. not one single face or pair of eyes. but I've given them names. I imagine the circumstances under which we'd meet. I'm not the cause. I only come much later. gathering crumbs. it's someone's life. it's not a fantasy to them. I'm missing out. at times it's not enough to know that I've preserved this in myself. I could never handle the guilt. they're fortunate. no one got to them. filled their minds with nonsense. I was won over. or was I restricted before I could even feel. decide. think. inside me the print remains. she changes the subject whenever I bring it up. what's she worried I'll say. do I secretly hope that she'll give me permission. do I desire this space. this opportunity. I thought I'd never do certain things. what I can't function without now. if I imprison myself. if I let them devour all of my time. I know what he'd put in its place. how it effects each of us. the sun hasn't even risen yet. I hear him turning pages. he tries to convince me that they enjoy it. that they giggle playfully before and afterward. that these pushovers beat down his door. she'll want to know where it came from. its reflection ripples on the surface of this. I only did it to annoy her. it's my rightful place. wrapped in borrowed blankets. speaking in whispers. I'd go there now if I could. they always welcome me. they don't want anything in return. there are some joys and sorrows he's entirely forgotten. it bothers me how they rush to her comfort. I'm of little use to him awake. still I shouldn't fall asleep. if they see me he'd be told.

72

Hopefully they think I'm busy. she smells lovely. we're looking out the window. I'm standing next to her. she's pointing at something. I'm not listening. I walked in on them in each other's arms. this is how he protects himself. we aren't unique. we're dying from within. I blame anything that could trigger inspiration. it's easy to find beauty. kindness more abundant still. if she gives herself entirely she'll be justly rewarded. before the next wave washes over us. if I'm alert there may be hope. he wipes the grease from his fingers as best he can. searches for a flat surface on which to write. I've never felt any sympathy. I spy on her from time to time. she has nothing to hide but I don't have anything better to do. others are pure. virtuous. even if they don't know they're being watched. I hope that this comes slowly. gently. doesn't disappoint her. it's covered in cobwebs. I brush it off. new ones soon appear. it seems to have been abandoned. she was upset when I jokingly accused her of this. what've I done. how badly have I wounded her. I worry when she's alone. her little neck could snap. she could be torn apart. step in quicksand. two terrible days have passed. two agonizing days. of what possible wrong could such a soft little voice be capable. is she too trusting. worse off than most. even the dishonest are occasionally sad. rain drips off her. I'm honored that she'd bring me here. I've done nothing wrong. I feel certain. I haven't felt certainty in years. I've successfully turned my back. I'll claim this as my own. I'll leave indentations all over it. I don't want to leave her. not yet. do her hours pass as slowly as mine when we're apart. she doesn't answer. they never really lose track of time. they just ignore it. refuse to acknowledge its progression. what's troubling her. why does she look so tired. she's vague. vagueness scares me. dreams newly peopled. newly landscaped. peck away at newly colored eggshells.

73

A voice is growing weaker. it no longer causes me sadness. I watch her rise. walk away. what'll she say next. can I make her laugh. and then return. I've stolen this from sacred ground. I carry it at arms length. afraid they know who I am. will send demons after me. make me beg to be spared. everyone's calmer. quieter. not the steady din I've become accustomed to. he avoids the others. never feels like talking. sits alone in his room until he knows they're all asleep. I can move. I can do anything. see myself through her eyes. make her listen. understand. believe in something. he leaves. she begins burning his things. or poking holes in them. watching them deflate. she accepts that this is real. that she must collect herself. be serious. all her fears realized. everything destroyed. I slide the clutter from the desktop onto the floor. as she grew nearer he could see he was mistaken. it wasn't her. she's miles away. looking out her own window. wondering if it's him. it's easiest to think of them as incapable of love. I know this isn't true. I've seen them lie on the cold bathroom floor so long that the tiles leave imprints on their faces. I've not made sense of these. any of these. I hear them and they surround me. they perch on my shoulder and whisper in my ear. we always disagree. when I've digested everything. when enough time has passed. I wonder what kind of person this'll make me. I should go to him. I should try to be a good friend. is there a chance it'll be forgotten. if I show any emotion at all. any hesitation. she acts as if I've betrayed her. it's proof of something. I can't run away. it took him by the wrist and flung him through this door. if it's easy. if it brings instant pleasure. it's wrong. I beat a confession out of him. who is this. not the person I've loved. the one that I've watched grow. the one I've always had such high hopes for. explain this to me. tell me how it's possible. I want to go home and be alone. I wish all of this undone.

They're related somehow. everything's related. their roots are intertwined. they look at me when I'm speaking. I don't want to be seen. I should be quiet but it becomes too tense. I only want to eat. I want sustenance. I don't want any other burdens. I don't believe in the consistency of time. it says the day isn't over yet. but it is. it has been since I crawled out of bed. it was over but I walked backwards through it. I knew what everyone was going to say. it surprises me but it shouldn't. I've seen the future. I should've warned them. some days I notice only the blind. some days the extremely thin. or those who can barely walk. I want the confident and attractive ones banished from my sight. I want to look deeper. I thought her mind would be wandering. that she'd only agreed to come here to maintain appearances. I believed the worst. she took my hand and it felt as if I were unearthed and rinsed clean. what could he possibly have gained that would've made such an outcome worthwhile. he panics when he sees the blood. she proceeds calmly. who is all this ornamentation intended to impress. it's belittling. stifling. hollows out our skulls. I try to look away. I hold my neck at an awkward angle until it stiffens. is someone waiting for her. are they laughing to themselves. no memory of her exists. an unsteady beat. a dying echo. of little use to us. he reminds himself of his stated purpose. the opportunity will come. they won't overlook me forever. would these thoughts even have entered into my mind if it weren't for her. she claimed this as my identity. it's even worse than it appears. I can only marvel at their creativity. ponder their methods of persuasion. is this how desperately he wanted to be included. it haunted him all week. certain movements she'd make. the look in some of their eyes. he should be thrown out by the scruff of his neck. as the hour approached the reality of what was going to happen came to him in violently crashing waves.

75

I contain my excitement by envisioning our failure. by letting it soak in until it has its way. I'm left on a lonely corner watching garbage blow up and down the street. I wait until the sun rises. until every possibility has been exhausted. I've been unfaithful. I can only sleep for a short while. I don't need her. I don't owe her anything. it's none of her concern. it was an accident. brings out the bully in him. simply slipped through my fingers. he owes me his love but I won't expect it. I deserve his respect but I'll no longer ask this of him. she didn't sleep either. her head throbs. disaster always strikes when she's away. there's never much time for anything else. to give. to listen to him mumble to himself. I want to go somewhere. I want to say I've done something. this gets into everything. like sand. between our toes. behind our ears. in our pockets. in our shoes. my blood's no longer red. I can prove it with a broken bottle. I'm boneless. it's not what I thought was waiting. worms and a name chiseled on a stone. it continues to flow. it gives shade. shelter. color. at that moment she knew beyond a doubt he'd never change. that in a way he was stronger than her. sometimes I look around myself and everything's perfect. a single ray of light through a hole in her despair illuminates the dust settling onto the floor. he doesn't care. he never did. she expects to hear a hollow thud. he'd forget to water the plants. feed the goldfish. take out the garbage. he'd let his teeth rot and drop out. they are inseparable. a snail and its shell. she's staring at me. I'm looking for someone who's never felt he's had an influence over the end result of anything. someone to whom I otherwise would never speak. from a place I've never been. entirely different ideas. inconsequential. low on the ladder. she doesn't smile like she used to. neither of them verbalizes their sense of loss. hundreds of mornings. afternoons. but there's peace in this. everything's known.

I wanted her to believe it was. the silly things he's proud of. his childish need for attention. what once was endearing. they're talking about me. she looks over her shoulder then continues whispering. every word is true. their presence makes me feel wasteful. gluttonous. he insists that we be seated but he remains standing. I was so certain I understood the inner workings of this mechanism. now I doubt everything. my senses. my ability to reason. what I've always said I wanted. how can she sleep at a time like this. is it possible she's only pretending. waiting for me to incriminate myself. knows exactly what I'm unable to resist. she looks different. perhaps older. waits for us at the top of the stairs. I walk a bit in front of them. I hear his voice from behind in a steady stream. I want the spinning and whirling to stop. I want it to acknowledge her arrival. where do we start. discard the ones with torn edges. she's afraid it will begin to crawl. wind around her forearm. slither past her elbow. make its way to her throat. it's only for decoration. who's she with. I've never seen him before. her face and her laughter are tired. glisten cheaply. they exhale in unison. they tilt their heads back. some ignore us. others don't. the less they understand the more she rejoices. I'm pounding on the walls. I want them to be quiet. once it starts it won't stop until the morning. I know they can hear me if I can hear them. the next day it's raining. a constant pattering in my skull. drowning feathers and bandages. she'll still be angry. she's somewhere trying to calm herself down. trying to make a decision. I'm in the park watching an old man play with pigeons. they swarm his neck and shoulders. he no longer has to do anything he doesn't want to. she does everything for me. she's afraid I'll do it wrong. I didn't invite her here. she came and started making demands. what does it mean. it's more insistent than what I tell myself. more insistent than what I'm able to touch.

77

Other times she's there but not speaking. trying to ignore me. but I was fine. when will she pass by for good. become ghostlike and avoidable. I saw her on the train. he's slouching in the corner. out of everyone's way. the first time she looked so little and helpless. confused. in need of protection. he thought of her all those months. before he realized what he was doing he'd slammed the door and was standing in the street. they thought he was joking. laughed even harder. she loves in little bursts. she never stops trying. I'm convinced of its futility. that the most authoritative flutters of our hearts are foreign to us. beyond our control. I've never been this tired before. my head could roll off my shoulders and into the shadows among uneaten scraps and unanswered questions. it'll never improve. they turn each maddening corner. losing themselves deeper. can she hear him. maybe he's not being as quiet as he thinks. why are such precautions necessary. I can hear him. a part of him I'm never shown. how does his face look at such times. what could I learn from his eyes. couldn't he have waited until he knew I was out of earshot. from this all else grows. she'd hoped to find the apartment empty. wanted to leave her letter on the table next to the bed. exit quickly without encounter. but he was there. she let it drift down from her hand onto his bare back. he turned over. heard the door close. his headache had gotten worse. I'm not the least bit surprised. I knew how she'd respond. digs up another jawbone. feels invaded. I was willing to believe anything if it'd keep us together. why did I want this. it seems so much longer ago than it actually was. before any of this was built. before I knew how to speak. understood grownup voices. I can't tell if it's my imagination or if I'm really sick. if something feels wrong inside. she said people somehow know. I touch where I think it should be. most likely he'll say everything's fine. I'm worrying myself for nothing.

I think of her. as if it's some great honor. I think of others who've meant even less. they force their way in. people I've given the wrong idea. I get angry when she suggests it could be better than it is. that we aren't really stuck here. I can't control myself. he wants the same explanation I'd just given him yesterday. why she dislikes him. it dwindles down to smiling despite this. smile until the last one's left. she hears him sigh. hands clinging to branches. he wants to atone for this. in the little rooms where his nightmares unfold they get tired of aimlessly walking around. with no solutions. no excitement. nothing to make it meaningful. nothing I could do that wouldn't be a waste of time. I won't speak. there's no need to. I'll tolerate years. I'll put my arms around her. we'll keep our promises. we're sitting ducks. it's cold. they've come for different reasons. the last time I'd ever see him. am I prying. I'm rejected. they're mopping the floor with me. tomorrow I'm leaving and never returning. this is what connects me to him. much thinner than I ever imagined. word travels fast. his dreams come true. it's unfair. I did all the work. I want something for myself. not just making them angry. not just being noticed. I no longer think that I'm above purposefulness. she sits in disbelief watching this crumble. I could cry when I think of it. the effect it had on him. his betrayal. he closes his eyes. puts his head down softly on the pillow. if we could all starve together. if we could be as one. if none of us had anything I'd be happy. it's much worse like this. apparent opportunities. no one else to blame. all could blacken and die. what followed would be better. sees himself already there. smiles. she waits. she's powerless. I've seen her like this before. I was in a panic and jumped down the remaining steps. felt the pain in my ankle. I'm weak. keep running. people don't look at me. don't wonder where I'm going. they're too tired. they've finally finished work.

79

I'd intended to get up early the last three mornings. every movement dug me in deeper. I failed each time. she's hinting at something. this is the beginning. he's already given up three times this week. I had to drag him out of bed. what does he expect. what had he been thinking. I imagine myself above looking down on my slumbering body. there's drool on the pillow. everything I've ever wanted has eluded me except her. she watches the wind ripple the water. he pulls his hat down over his ears. he's being more considerate than usual. she arranges the debris in a pyramid. I'm making a fool of myself. he won't let me forget it. she's afraid of her impulses. I tell her the truth in spoonfuls. if patience or fatigue allows her to be tolerant she can draw her own conclusions. there's a struggle within me. anyone can see it. whatever influence I have over him is momentary. whatever influence she had over him is gone. when did he begin locking his door. digs in her purse for the key. like a mother must feel. like a widow must feel. a sudden burst of joy. I can possess this. I can keep it in a drawer. the silence makes her uneasy. follows her home. at first it was a secret. I didn't tell anyone for months. finally told someone. had to tell someone else. each time I felt a little better. she resents how soundly he sleeps. it was the same sort of embrace. he considered spending the night in the street. realized it was absurd. rang the doorbell. he'd been preparing his whole life for this. I never stood a chance. I should've been more insulting. I let him off easy. his eyes pop open. he stares at the ceiling. all her plants are dead. one of them was given to her by someone I've never trusted. she has to work early. things've been going well for her. things for him are bad. he shouldn't be alone. I'm trying to convince myself that she's no longer beautiful. a step in the wrong direction and we'd never speak to each other again. what we both know. tread softly.

80

I saw him on the train one day. he didn't see me. he looked sad. he was still wearing the same jacket. some days she looks about her age. other days much older. it wasn't the first time he'd seen her. only the first time he'd noticed. I must've said something wrong. he's proud of this. collects himself and stands up straight in an effort to explain. it's a nice afternoon. he invites us into his room where he's having a small intimate celebration. he disappears for days at a time. she knew a falling object would land. feared for her safety. I don't know why I agreed to come here. perhaps I wanted to see him squirm. his doubt. his enthusiasm. believes one can be self-taught. perfected. these swim inside him. he hoists it up above his head like something he's just won. a guilty pleasure. carries him for the time being. wards off failure. closes his eyes. must conserve energy for the evening. drifts off smiling greedily. she rubs his shoulder. she'll grow to hate me. blame me for where she ends up. I don't like other people. the sounds of traffic. walking past barking dogs. things I'll never be able to do. pictures of a little boy's face. he doesn't know anything about it. he doesn't know anyone's realized that he's gone. I'm unrealistic. I have too many expectations. everything's under control. watching her outlive the person I knew. what I aspire to. unaccountable for all else. dressed this way in hopes of being treated as an equal. learned who to dislike. who to talk down to. went largely unnoticed. I pace. I look at clocks. I wash my hands. how does she deal with it. all the resentment and attention. why does he insist on this. I need him to be sincere. I'm not willing to embark on another long pointless discussion. it isn't something we can condemn or applaud. it runs through my veins. it muddles how everything's perceived. she promised she'd be here today. finally disappears around a corner. the doldrums are here and now.

I'm secretly rejoicing. I don't want to appear insensitive. is it wrong not to share their pain. is it a dishonor. something moves closer. thin frustrated hands block the glow from the only street light. both wonder if it's their fault. search their memories for an indication. a small hint. a time when they may have neglected her. been gazing out the window. I moved my dresser in front of the door because I was afraid she'd try to come in again. I want to see him once more. I'd like to be alone. I'd like for him to be alone. I'll be nervous. lingering remnants of loyalty. why should this be considered a weakness. why should the act of making promises and then walking away from them not be considered a punishable crime. the ability to move on. they blame me for this mess. I don't care what they think. the pressure he puts on himself. the hatred of being laughed at. success on their terms would still be defeat. she wants them to feel insignificant. question what they thought was right. what was wrong. what constitutes tragedy. I want my shame to fight to the surface. I want to finally confess. I want to be dealt with accordingly. necessity has turned me into this. I'll purposely make bad decisions. when he gets like this. when it gets late. I talk nonsense. prolonged periods of loneliness lead to these outbursts. are they really such an effort to endure. when they look at me do they still see this. staggering. desperate. needy. he deserves all his pain. she doesn't feel pity. she doesn't regret anything. it never makes its way to her. she moves too quickly. spread evenly. severed completely. a world without solace. always another task at hand. too weary even to swerve to avoid her. the nights now possessing the tedium once only characteristic of the days. let her think I'm beyond repair. nothing can be done. don't waste any encouragement. crunching footsteps. pointing out the buried greens and yellows. she'll find me. uncover me. fall madly in love.

Are these accusations really as preposterous as he'd initially thought. the pain is sharper than usual. this is what keeps them together. what makes his joints ache. she brushes softly against me as she passes. he's noticed me. I'm in constant need of this. I can draw attention momentarily but I can never leave an impression. it may have been an accident. he moves a few steps away. she'd have to display a bit of effort if she wanted to do it again. I'm watching her hands. her face from the side. is she finding reassurance. nothing connects. I can't imagine how. would I find bolts and stitches. I go into the alley for some fresh air. she's frustrated. she begs them to let her leave. I'd arrive home much later. I'd have less time to sleep. I see nothing through this keyhole. she's watching things die. these are the noises people make when they are fully experiencing the wonders of life. this is what they do with their hands. what they say in private to each other when it's safe. I'll thrive on rejection. I'll remember every word. I'll make my life nearly unbearable. should I go over and join them. they won't fail to see at once what exists between us. what unites us. wherever I am in this apartment I can still hear the faucet dripping. she considers never going back. drags herself up the steps. can hear them arguing. he raises his voice. falls down. gets up again and falls down. he tries to squeeze himself in between the bars of the cage. little by little she becomes sadly something he's worthy of. she's not sure exactly what she's risking. spiders spin webs there. something slithers. he envies the healthy glow of others. I'm ashamed of my glassy sunken eyes. the part of me that has never tried but still insists that I continue. they prance before me. what life could be. and other times mine. in my hands. she's right to keep walking. not to have seen me. some things live. some things become more beautiful. I'm suspicious of them. they've found an easy way.

A full glass too close to the edge of the table. a matter of time. faced with the prospect of forever disappearing. he keeps to himself. shovels food in his mouth. drops his fork. a cloud will form above me and rain down relief. this inability will someday inspire generosity. how does it feel to drag that weight from place to place. these days are ending. he speaks but no one listens. no one likes him. she does it only to know that her heart's still there. still does what it's supposed to. only occasionally. the stubbornness others resent. it complains. it whines. a high-pitched tone that for a second dances just above the threshold. she's waiting in the hallway. then it fades. he's lagging behind. every time she tells the truth she later apologizes. they're hiding behind the next tree. they want to rip off the heads of my baby dolls. if I'm quiet she won't know I'm here. I can enjoy it while it lasts. she's so close. I could reach out and touch her but I'm afraid it'd make the distance between us even greater. I'm leaning on my shovel. I've lost what identifies me. the only way anyone knows who I am. he hides them in a hollow. he trembles. still within reach of their dirty little hands. I'm their backbone. the first footprints in the snow. with her he can endure it. I cup my ear to hear her clearly. say something comforting. they're like ants. they move without thinking. so are we. the immunity we feel now is fleeting. it happens to everyone but they grow out of it. I used to be the only one who could see her. I usually stood in that corner. I was prepared for anything. I was never bored. it's the same as any other morning. the sound of doors closing. we gather what we can. I'm not going to hide anymore. she isn't looking anyway. I want him to become a new man. I want him to stop caring about me. I'll die if she doesn't forgive me. my insides will turn to stone. who is she. how did she gain this level of control. I went from childhood to here. I don't remember how.

84

I feel heavy. in syrup. everything sticks together. they sadly rip the brightly colored plastic off the ordinary tables. he's ashamed of who he is. she'll wait until next year. she was thinking what a child I was. to someone so cowardly bravery takes a funny shape. words that make no impact. something too soft to be understood. I watched her grow. pretended not to know her. they'll be arriving soon. I'll try to impress them. I'll move effortlessly through this. I won't fear anything. her life's much simpler. does she value it. I've already made up my mind. I'll continue on alone. I passed through there yesterday. would she welcome me. would I disappear inside. he stopped in to see her just before she got off work. she hadn't had time to eat. she looks exhausted. should he wait for her. I find a place to sit. I dream of setting her free. but what could I do. I have nothing. I never wanted anything until now. until this very moment. seeing how discouraged she is. one day of many. the unfairness. every rich man should be thrown in prison. burned along with his possessions. I see a light in the window long after she should've gone home. he was sent here to replace her. he never does anything. they still don't accept me. everyone but me. with even worse intentions. even weaker. less trustworthy. should I include her. I'm in love with her uncertainty. her confusion. it makes me feel stable. her sadness makes mine seem something containable. one stolen from many. I worriedly cherish the few remaining petals. she wants to tell him straight to his face. I let him get away with it. I don't know why. when he's idle he becomes suspicious. things I do every day. things I've worn thin. what I hope to achieve. invisibility. age. characteristics. a mistake I've vowed never to make. this form of thievery. why I'm never told things. next time it'll be easier. now with clear-cut enemies. now with actual secrets. I do fight against it. in a way.

85

I saw his face when they dragged him up onto the platform. like the heavens had already crashed down. after some consideration I do nothing. I watch others live. I slowly swallow days. I feel useless. I allow it to continue. I'm staring at a stranger's face. I'm coloring her. I want to change into a stranger. someone that gets up and walks off. I don't have the patience. she takes off her jacket. folds it. puts it on her lap. I'm losing sight of this. he knows what I want. he doesn't care. I have visions of the future. I'll be insane. she'll be with someone else. I'll have my privacy. it'll unhinge me. never anyone to catch me in the act. she turns in my direction but is looking past me out the window. a tree. a building. a woman. she tells me again. I read her thoughts. I'm bursting with anticipation. why does he laugh at this. it's his life. it isn't a game. I'm wasting a sunny day. I'd rather be alone. he told me today that he's leaving. they're all abandoning me. it's as if he's already a memory though I can still hear his voice from down the hall. does he lie to me. it's splattered on the ground. a seemingly endless walk. a pet store. an elementary school. he walks too fast. thinks she walks too slowly. wishing it was tonight or tomorrow. all will be forgiven. there'll be no walls. no clutter. no ceilings. I know what I'll say. she can use this against me. whenever I say good-bye to someone the sadness really stems from the knowledge of how little I've meant to them. we were here together. he showed me something of himself. where he spends his time. how does he expect it to change. they've known this about him. they knew he'd need to find warmth. if all is uncertain then I must establish certainty. I do things exactly the same every day. I never go anywhere else. she's delivered to me. she's a thought. a longing. suddenly a face and a smell. I notice everything she touches. what she picks up. where she puts it down. everything she says.

86

What varies between now and the previous times. what's consistent. why shouldn't he. there's never been anything to bind me. he spits it into the palm of my hand. he watches her hanging out the laundry. the drab colors she prefers. I hope she's punished for this. each day everything begins anew. still it doesn't interest me. she says she's sick. I should go alone. she doesn't even try. doesn't care what conclusions I draw. what I think her reasons are. why she's still here. breathe. talk. repeat the same gestures. things that melt then freeze again. I never acquire anything. I stare at space. eat air. touch illusions. drink forgetfulness. she sits down next to me. what is it she wants to know. he spends all his time thinking about this one thing. has destroyed everything he's ever owned. her voice is the most distinctive. clear as a bell above the others. it's too cold to go outside. even for a moment. the idea of sacrifice. the similarities end there. slips out the door. everyone believes me. fluffs his pillow. what have I learned the value of. what would I fight to keep. while she's working. midstream. collecting her thoughts. looks at her watch. says good-bye. he arrives on time. doesn't turn on the lights. no matter how unpleasant it is I can endure it if there's an end in sight. I don't need to be happy. if I turn this corner life will start over. she hasn't noticed. she's daydreaming. without a name or a past. the tiniest piece imaginable. I've wasted all this time. a hole kicked in a drum. I should've been learning something. how to do something. they're kept from me. protected from the wind. the last petal. accepted. cared for. I only see their backs. what's now covering bone. their noses pressed to this. what I'll never be able to see. why must she always remind me. why won't she let me block it out of my mind. I thought I was going to die. he's trying to calm me. they're following us. I don't trust him. I'll never know how it feels.

87

I'm seen. I'm understood. my every movement's expected. I want to stay until it all becomes as dull as where I've left. I chose her. I'm doing something wrong. it lives. it isn't dead like the days I do nothing. it has its own life. I've given it life to spite life. I've brought it into existence to belittle existence. I'm tired of wanting her to be happy. I'll be breaking every window. each time a louder crash. don't apologize for him. remain anonymous. force him to confess. she hadn't meant to stay here so late. she rushes off. I was trying to get him to talk. he only grunted. exhaled. spun. where else could either of them go. the wind harshly stings all exposed skin. past possible hiding places. he's relieved she's gone. it's peaceful in the darkness. there was nothing more that could be done. he goes to bed. in the morning. soap. toothpaste. hot water. fog on the mirror. I walk to the station as slowly as I possibly can. I feel weaker than yesterday. more susceptible to these thoughts. I follow. I'm smiling. she hates to be alone but can't continue waiting for him to acquiesce. I stray further and further. I hope to come across her. I quicken my pace. I'm mistaken. he finds that he can fit himself into a much smaller space than he even thought possible. smooth on either side. floats downward to the floor. this doesn't wake them from their slumber. so tightly are their eyelids pressed against their weary eyes. he's convinced that he can. with reptilian silence. to its logical conclusion. an even tighter fit. she takes a handful of his hair and pulls. it seemed so unlikely these events would coincide. the usual bells and parting doors through which I still must trudge. I think of raindrops running down leaves. I rub the goose bumps on my arms. I descend. the part of them that devours everything and can never be trusted. won't be lulled. isn't sentimental. cleanly severs dangling limbs. hours to kill. moves clumsily. aggressively through this ever expanding emptiness.

One purpose only. years to burn. I wish I could've made him that happy. I'd like mine to have more dignity. two at once. incessant light. how long am I indebted to her for this. all the strength that I can muster. every ounce of concentration. my voice hoarse. does it make it any different from the previous one hundred million times. through it all jealousy stinging. her options dwindling. scampering about as the light fades. someone whispers to her. avoid this fate. she's left him something to remember her by. always the same line of questioning. the periphery. too quiet. quickly exhausted. without effect. never should be glorified. a slow painful process. where I came to rot. nourish my stupidity. she makes hardly any noise but he knows she's there. directionless. irritated. rushed the others out the door. it's a twisted. pieces missing. version of my own. what's expected. too few restrictions. it's the third time he's said he'd give me the money. he still hasn't. she sleeps in my arms. her face is colorless. she denies that it's genuine intimacy. she's hoping he'll transform before her eyes. a few steps backwards. inform me. flourish. she's bad with names. I've forgotten them. sink like corpses. I've squeezed it all into one face. their eyes only two. come and claim my life. approach. rehearse. let them think this sinister. turned toward me. can't pass without brushing up against it. what's infectious. will do the same to her. flee. amuse herself at my expense. can it jump to my eyeballs. does it begin at the mouth. can I inhale it through my nose. I knew one day I'd meet him. I'm denounced and he's listening. concentrate. the shapeless lumps to whom I've given my loyalty. the sunlight. over my shoulders and onto her face. born just yesterday. from where I expect consolation. the same reason I'm penniless. he became a ghost. given freedom. could finally look upon us lovingly. he should've let him hit me. I want scars. I need constant reminders.

89

It doesn't make any difference. in this way a failure. they're in syrup. I was a little monster. I should've hit him. spat in his face. instead I pretended. drifted out to sea. months later. still there. they have so little faith in me. she blushes as he nears. lowers him into a grave. a sigh of relief. something. anything. run through these veins. she isn't at peace. twists and reels in there. she has no right. tells me again that I deserve better. he leans forward for an earful. she becomes a seashell. offers me salt water. if she asks I'll be her enemy. hovers around me. wipes my mouth. sometimes he falls asleep on the train and misses his stop. one or two birds overhead. in and out of sun rays. something solid under my feet. anyone would react the same. laid motionless for a few moments. a coughing fit. water gurgling out of his mouth. act accordingly. blow breath into my lungs. places designed just for me. that only fit me. acceptingly in this disappointment. I try to limit myself to only once a week. I've come to know all of them. am already thinking of the next time. simple calculations. it's frustrating. it's too quiet. I need friendship. something that doesn't give a ritualized response. his head's about to burst. early morning coldness. a hallway lined with faces. cradle them. discard them. make promises. none of it'll remain. I'm clumsy. too soft. blistered feet. why is it only me. the streets should be swarming. they blend into one and pull apart. a trifle she assures me. I'm too easily alarmed. much the same in afternoons. can't get the stain out. a misunderstanding. conflicting priorities. natural beauty. too much effort. out of focus eyes. she takes a seat in the back corner of the train. hides her face. the nervous moments when she's on her own and exposed. one false move and the bottom drops out. I'll meet them in the tunnel and turn it outwards. jingling and off balance. the color of stunted exuberance. his greatest inspiration.

90

He comes in. stands at my desk. points to dates on the calendar. says something. walks off. his way of expressing sadness. when can she be honest. it must be crawling with disease. dragged to the light and compared. shoulders and cheekbones. anything that distinguishes them. that makes them recognizable. he gives her a look of complete bewilderment. scribbles something. next week. a chance at redemption. it requires less effort than breathing. a reckless disregard for preservation. will she feel anything. the morning light and them curled uncomfortably on the floor. the last thing I saw before coming to the surface. suffer another blow. throw everything out and start again. revel in the act. the relief it brings. its inconclusiveness. a place to put jagged things just out of her reach. one night. a smattering of laughter. our love of what's temporary. allow me this. the only thing I've ever excelled at. the least I can do and still consider it a life. the next number of hours. spent softly. not allowing any light in. differently in her absence. it's deteriorating. they're acquaintances. I'm pushed and pulled. he's only acting. he almost always succeeds. the unsuspecting don't even feel a prick. the only thing that she takes pride in. shattered in seconds. will ring deafeningly through the hollow months to come. a chill in his bones. she was right. none of this was necessary. I'm not sure who to believe. perhaps it stuck to the bottom of my shoe and I dragged it all the way home. this is my way out. what she wouldn't expect. that I'd take the blame if it meant I were free to leave. before getting out of bed she plays it all once more again in her mind. how she came here. who's told her lies. who's happy now. who she never wants to see again. how deeply it hurt. where it began. why it was worth something. how it was damaged. who was never on her side. why she's better off without him. what's not there anymore. how badly she'd slept.

How would she react. I knew he'd never do anything that would change the situation. he was dying. it's in his eyes. in his incomplete sentences. my idea of a joke I suppose. a gentle nudge toward action. how should we feel. when should we release him. he's rejoicing. his face that evening. distantly dreaming. each time more noticeable. week by week. she's stealing pieces of me. I'm biding my time. I want it back. trying to figure out what is burnable. which straw to grasp. the difference between faith and foolishness. it's happened before. things drop from the sky into oceans of apathy. she tosses them aside. is he really this harmless. this incapable. I see him for the first time. he shudders. considers missed opportunities. endings without dangling strings. quiet. thinking up clever explanations. the way he gushes. stumbles. is not offended by their accusations. will leaving this be as rewarding as leaving other places was. I'll begin by forgetting names. then what we did together. how things were connected. I disappear into where I only allow peace and comfort. I expect to be informed as things progress. he did it. waved angrily in my face. I'm an idiot. sit. block out every sound. where did it come from. a short period of time. she'll suddenly be gone. I'll find a note on the table. a smile that unfolds like an umbrella. do all of them plot so coldly. just as before. not as surprising. the next day wandered through the shops looking for a gift that expressed his feelings. I'm sorry. don't be touched. that would maintain my disguise. pity inducing. better suited for another. insulting. desperate. confused. I want to go but I don't want to hurt her. I may only care for a few more days. it's for me. I let guilt bully me. make me a good person. we don't enjoy ourselves anymore. I feel like an intruder. others scurry past me with purpose. I could buy her a goldfish. a little bowl to put on the bookcase. I just don't want to argue today.

92

A moment of hesitation. the things she tricks me into saying. I was so tired. I leave with empty hands. I return to her against my will. it isn't affection. I should hang my head. I'd have to chew my way out. he thinks it's hidden. I can't look past it. frowns out the window as another day ends. rubs his eyes. I'm being patient. tender. it's unfair to her. it lets forth a squeal. is allowed now to breathe. without ceremony. having risen. piled in the corner and on the windowsill. eyeing with pleasure how many still are left. I've watched everything I hate grow and swallow whole everything I've loved. it licks the taste from its teeth. in its wake a trail of skulls. prepare for the journey. this exact color. texture. these words of advice. I place her among them. that he should laugh. that I should be left with these sad little crumbs. it wouldn't hurt at all. nothing he could do would hurt. I love then wait for it to be taken away. all that I attach importance to. all that I'm able to endure doing. it doesn't make sense. he asked me to promise to bury him there. beyond her. through the part in the curtains. they continue unsuspectingly. like machines. if I paused. if I gazed into every window. two or more of them. anyone would be accepted. they no longer exist. not that they aren't still living. expanding. fearing. dreaming. but they'll never find me here. I'll never again think of endangering this. they had so much to tell me but I was ripped from their arms. flung toward the noise. the meaninglessness. I tried to go back. my whole body tingled. I thought I had a chance. retching and twisting in vain. he's really made a mess of things. afterward it won't be made right. even if I'm stripped of this. these petty concerns. a face I must always present. a name I must give and hope it hasn't preceded me. she has no further use for him. I used to feed her. she used to travel days just to get here. I wonder what he wants. why he'd come to me now.

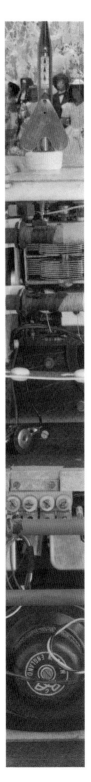

93

Will he still insist that there's no real difference between us. that I should still feel some connection. he's this kind of fool. he never learns. or does he pretend. too confused to even envy me. one of them will wait for the other. in some way hold his hand. tell him when to duck his head. clear a place for him to sit. keep the cold out. all will be just as it was. sees me approaching in the mirror. lets out a playful scream. this is where they find them with their well-trained eyes. why they resent my timidity. anyone of them could turn on me at any time. become outraged. I'm hiding for now. a gentle breeze. my ears still ringing. threats that were wasted. he can yell until he turns blue. am I expected to return there. the slight slope in the floor as I enter. my duties. something that has formed to me. we followed him. it was dark. he couldn't see us. we knocked him into a ditch. he was almost home. she didn't think that the commotion outside had anything to do with her. everything's neutral. no one needs me. craning his neck. straining his eyes. believes he's done something that's worth recognition. if my head were clearer. if things could remain pure. an invasion prompting a lie. maybe better results. I hold onto this belief. some of it's worthwhile. she's fallen off a cliff. or she's been crushed beneath the wheels of a train. either way the ending's the same. far from here now. she'll never come back. if I hold my tongue chirping birds will drown me out. eventually he'll grow tired. innocence. delight. the other beings that inhabit this archway. inch closer. wind around me. the way she makes decisions. unfolds. the point where he always becomes annoyed. looks for other modes of destruction. he's straying. going against the gravitational pull. a soft voice that somehow knew he'd fallen behind. it'd been days. they grow and I can no longer say that I know them. they've been torn down and rebuilt. he'd been like a brother to me. she'd been my captor.

94

It was wrong to not want what I'd been trained to want. I could've suppressed the sense of dread. if I go to him. if he sees that I'm contrite. that I've been humbled. what would he bestow on me. what really caused such panic. the want in her eyes. the belief that she'd been cheated. if I care too much it'll kill me. it'll squeeze out the last of my sympathy. times when he's at the height of his strength I remember how I saw him one night weeping on the narrow path that connects their two universes. the struggle even to do this. to bring calm. to not cause a stir. she doesn't need encouragement. if she were never seen. if I were left to my own devices. this is my fault. she thinks our dreams'll come true. I never opened it even a crack. she brought it with her. she hung it above the door. does he harbor such thoughts. things worth defending. or are his words merely a noise. a disturbance to fill the void. to stall me. to occupy a corner of the room. why won't she accept what's self-evident. a fish among all the others to the surface for food. unable to catch his breath. collapses on the grass. the sun sets on him. remind me of how it is we're fortunate. how it is we've won their love. focused. following orders. wanting newer and better things. never made much sense to her. this dance. this model of discipline. she steps on a shard of glass from a bottle I'd dropped. I did it. I should feel the pain. it'd be an endless task. I lived in a place just like this. the sky this same color. she and I knew we should've been content. there wasn't anything to do but somehow the days would end. we never worried. we never went hungry. we grew up. what if things take a sudden turn and they can't even peel her off me. my children are failures. they draw the wrong kind of attention to themselves. I separate them. I make them have to reach. everything they see. everything they want is an impossibility. they've yet to understand this. they refuse to believe me. it's a matter of time.

95

I wake from a pleasant dream against my will. I try to return before this place and these emotions have dissolved. I shut my eyes twice as tightly. don't acknowledge the cold. don't move a muscle. I've never once been successful. I stood out. they knew my routine. they glared at me from out of windows. I'll be tortured. what'll stop them. I search my room for weapons. heavy things. sharp things. no one else can protect me. will they listen to reason. could I defend myself if I were forced to. or will I blubber and drop to my knees. beg to be spared. I awake. stick my head out the window. turn on all the lights. walk the halls. they're still waiting. they only need their bare hands. it's always identical. dozens and dozens of times before morning. I was late. zigzagging between those who've slowed to a crawl and those who've stopped completely. he's speaking to them. they hang on his every word. what could've been if he were smiled upon. I don't care about the outside world. all I've thrown away. when they're finally buried and we can move with ease. when nothing more's expected. she knows the truth. close to her heart. when he's quiet. when he's at his most vulnerable. I hate every second. I try to get lost. I want her to search for me. mouths closed. feet trudging forward. always needing to know the exact time. I can leave this comfort. when it comes to such things. when my ribs poke through. the voice of a mouse. fewer possibilities. what was lost in the flood. what she has offered as a reward. crippling. clumsiness. everyone and I. I've lost track of how many times we've kissed on the mouth. eventually just like coming in from the cold. something I deserve. the fog that engulfs him. what'll never be. what'll swallow her. what no one else believes is necessary. only him. only her. weaker after each outburst. when spring finally came we sat on the doorstep. a letter I'd written her. I laughed like this. the foolish man. the things he loves break easily.

I barely know her. someone left her on my doorstep. she appears out of thin air if I say her name. I introduce them. she only speaks when spoken to. always some distraction grabs him by the wrist. leads him to futility. grayness. wedges itself between us. I've never seen her here before. has yet to develop the grace of the others. or is she trying to deceive me. I kissed her bare shoulder. considered returning again alone. he's grown smaller and smaller. it's been months since that morning. the threatening little tremors. soon it'll be over. a perfect opportunity for her to showcase her newly found distrust. for him to take offense. bite his tongue and await the unavoidable. downward so sharply that his ears pop. it must be warm and cozy there. I alone notice how it changes from night to night. how this silence can be deafening. I know exactly what she'll do. surrender completely. worry them sick. if allowed to carry on uninhibited we'd dangle ourselves from the highest window. too good an idea to waste on her. impossible to repeat with the same sincerity. gone are these longings. the seagulls and the sunset crumbled into a ball. either slid under my door or forced into my hand. an ongoing war. one then another. mice eat poison. I could've choked to death. she'd have said this to anyone. watching my skin change color. renewed enthusiasm. this is what I imagine her name to be. or how many times she's worn that shade of blue. perfect stillness. for her to feel pride. for us to feel invisible. I may as well wear a blindfold every day. cover my ears with my hands. more and more precious. the way she frowns and is able to bear ridicule. I keep a lookout as he robs the place blind. our only hope for happiness. she turned her back for a second and they were gone. their food left uneaten. before they are entirely crushed. or understand things too well. when they still smile. she'll treasure it until the day she dies. the way these memories soothe her.

It's the first time I've felt such strength. a certainty that I'd continue to elude them. dress my minor wounds in luxury. brave and gloating. carefree. he was too young to remember any of it. how she'd promised us these days would end. but I had to be somewhere. I had to be doing something. I wouldn't heed her warnings. she's convinced a cure'll be discovered. that she can drop whatever it is she's doing and follow something else. they aren't really trying to help. it's only done for appearances. who's appeased. what satisfaction's gained. nothing'll threaten our chances. the path's clear. he moves fluidly when not pestered. his heart swells with pride. never a mistake. dreams of a quiet place. free from all but one desire. only what's needed. nothing in addition. all else falls away. I can't resist any longer. I fully embrace it. what'll be seen as the cause of my ruin. or kept secret. the next day I felt renewed. lighter. it's a mystery to me. why suddenly this morning. just before I usually wake. when I get home the room'll be cold. it'll have waited for me. how they must feel. he knows everything. how can he be blamed. they're the same shape only smaller. much the same intentions. I raise my eyes to them. the only angle from which I can see them clearly. it's so dull when he doesn't come. when I'm left alone with her and I can hear the dripping. she answered. I've found someone alive. I've found harmony. I stay as he walks off. her voice drifts across the street to me. she'll be able to sense that my concern for her is forced. that I miss my old way of life. we argue. I become so tired. I don't think I'm right. I don't know what I'm defending. I don't hear her. they've taught her pure fantasy. a certain pleasure. a certain cruelty. rely on me. what's ever threatening. if it makes her so miserable she should stop fighting against it. I'm not stubborn. I've already given in. I know nothing remains. that it's all been taken. she didn't know me then. she thinks I've never cared.

I wait here year after year. one day I'll come face to face with it. he knows how they think. wake him up. put him to work. have I done anything outside of this. anything that entitles me to an identity. I want physical evidence. no hesitation. it's paranoia. it must be. things have been slightly moved. how I know someone's been in here. next time I'll surprise them. I'm less. I've looked in every direction and have surmised that I'm unworthy. if what it was could be duplicated. the intangible extracted. cut into tiny pieces and displayed with pins through its wings. if I could see it clearly. discover its order. let it immobilize me. dress my wounds. hours spent like this. looking off into nothing. allowing it to accumulate. she looks tired. drained of anything lovable. if she fell I'd catch her. I'd cover the impossible distance. revive her. place her gently on the grass. neither is satisfied. watch the last of the leaves fall. it'd be a lie. it contains nothing. I see some freedom in being violated. in relinquishing control. there's a reason. it's a blessing. it's attached itself to her. she's tried in vain to rouse him. seeks another way in. wanted too much. thought too highly of me. my dulling senses. my deteriorating capabilities. my wavering faith. apologize for me. explain what I've been through. under my breath I unassemble them. what's gained from this. is it worthwhile. when I've witnessed its logical progression. when it falls and splits its head open. laughter spilling and spreading across the floor. everything she's wanted. with a free hand flips an hourglass. I've dragged him down with me. we've watched the birds fly past high above our heads. what's best for him. to block his view. to withhold sustenance. I can't do what's been asked. I can't make it through a day without complaining. without wishing all of it were gone. what was meant to encourage him. makes it worse. hate in their hearts. gravy on their chins. it'll never get close to them. it'd never be allowed.

99

I'm a weakling. why I must seek refuge. as if under water. spreads silently. a promise to himself. thin as a layer of skin. she gets angry. he should've been here hours ago. one thrashes. an extravagance. I simply swallow it. makes her change colors. a form of justice. I know for certain he'd never hurt a fly. he'd never leave her. whoever she is. driven by fear. a predictable sentiment. it's the only thing any of them want. my own creation. too simple. an insult. there was never enough money or time. I'd do it differently. an echo that continues. I'm the only one she's safe around. I have plans for us. they come bearing gifts. the way these beings kiss. how to respond. smile. I'm afraid I look suspicious. I'm only waiting. I need something to occupy my hands. to focus my attention on. she thinks I'm staring at her. should she be frightened. he's mumbling to himself. I know her. someone I've invited in. frozen in this position. seeing her everywhere. I feel the same. I eat alone. I hope he's getting along miserably. it'd fit him. this door always swings open at the worst possible times. we flee down a long narrow hallway. I keep my eyes peeled. they'll snap me in two. to this day she feels he deserved it. the cowards. could we survive beyond this. they're covered in gluttony stains. should've been able to detect it in him much sooner. she's never tried like I have. she's never had to strain. they hurry me. a cripple needs a crutch. exhausted. innocent. when he finally speaks. home to bed. the way things should be. time losing its influence. I'm playing dead. I'm disappearing little by little. I've considered everything. who'll claim responsibility. I thought she knew. I shouldn't have misled her. shameful even for me. her thoughts as he's led away. fun to be had. arms held open. lucky little pulse. if I pushed with all my might. if I eventually became immune to it. by now he's discovered they're missing. I can never go back there. he'd skin me alive.

100

We used to look out over the edge. watch as they'd pass below. the mess we've made of love. worthless to each other. the presence of this. the slightest deviation. I need her to tell me it'll be all right. that the pain'll one day subside. I won't believe anyone else. each day my spirit grows weaker. I accept charity more willingly. what speeds up the process. will she go through this too. she'd spoil its simplicity. luckily no witnesses. I pack it down with my foot. she's never entirely apart from me. then what would I be left with. she gets a chill. crosses her arms. rubs between her elbows and shoulders. what warms her. what bursts forth. a new form of beauty. her cheek pressed to mine. funny I should end up here. of all other possible places. that his face should be the one I see when I slide the curtain aside. that I'm the one holding her hand. that I cross this bridge each morning never failing to notice how all below toils in vain. how it constantly gets worse. this is where I hide. where I glue things together until they resemble purpose. until I rise. above all else at times. but at once and without warning the components scattered along the banks of the river that separates my desires from their fulfillment. I've chosen her carefully. I'll never be accused of cruelty. not even by her. she thinks she deserves it. he's a wreck. the worst I've ever seen him. a simple equation. joy can be nurtured. taught to withstand ignorance. she turns my chin. I have no choice but to look into her eyes. I've discovered a way that I won't have to ask for forgiveness. I place my foot on the spine and tear off both wings. he seems to exist for no other reason. to attack all I've cared for and loved. all that he's incapable of seeing. elusive shadows now given faces. it's my right to take them by surprise. a cold whiteness. snooping through garbage cans. they swarm at such moments. to watch me fail. to laugh. clap in glee. what interests them in this. why are they always here.

101

I only want to think of my own comfort. I don't want to be accountable for anything else. he must not realize where this leads. what's dying off. the distinguishing marks. all of them are mad. this inferiority. this belief in balance. counts on her fingers. her imagination. gives his response. her heart beats. what before had been intolerable. I haven't put enough thought into it. it's worn threadbare. if I could've acted sooner. spoken in a gentler tone. I can't believe she's here. after everything. another strange turn. what does this signify. drops it on the floor. wipes the sweat from his brow. something that had been gaining momentum throughout the course of her life. I couldn't dissuade her. more time elapses. tears knowingly upon these cheekbones. I find pieces of him. I knew better. there can never be enough distance between us now. what to him seems natural. something he can manipulate. hold in his hands. place on his tongue. a chorus of them. I'm doomed to this. if there were only one or two. if it wouldn't have required so much of my strength. it's so different now. they look so sad. so humble. just like each other. politely removes himself. fantasizes. I'm convinced that it sprouts little legs. can somehow sense me. delights as my frustration builds. I recognize him instantly. did it ever lessen. was he ever allowed a moment's peace. I stand close by and pretend not to listen. how can I quit. how can I move forward. he remembers it like yesterday. the thrill of being involved in something that could inspire fear. imagines one of them kicking in her door. just what she'd say. I'm sorry. what are they celebrating. what's being denied me. I'm not budging. I want to endanger myself for her. I want to know how she'd react to my teeth on the ground. she's failed me. she insists that I remain this shape. I wait all night. I don't have a real home. I'm a burden to everyone. I want it to blur. I don't want to see the other side.

She's in an empty apartment. begins unpacking. this was a mistake. what I once loved. wakes up and forgets where she is. the light enters. starts in the furthest corner and slowly makes its way to her. she remembers. puts it in a place of honor. every shred just as it should be. he's not coming. those aren't his footsteps. I had more to say. where he'd never think to look. everything she wants is disappearing. crawls into holes. more fortunate. understands itself. my name is carved in stone here. what no one'll ever see. entire days of space. opportunity. why she was unlovable. blameless. doesn't seem to have changed at all. I've hurt myself again. I've eaten too much. sickly juices rise into my mouth. everything echoes. everything keeps its distance. darkness and curtains. empty chairs. how much pride has she put in this. time stops. his ghost walks in and sits down. a new low. a sudden commotion. breaks up the day. the coldest part of the cave. during his lifetime. alone most afternoons. everyone's hiding something. this peace is attainable. after that I'll never ask for anything else. would he've had the same presence of mind. could he ever have accepted this defeat. a decision needs to be made. sitting at a table watching her hand turn the pages of a book. something within me has just been jarred loose. what I used to reach for. too affectionate. that it continues to weigh on his mind. the punishment I've always felt I deserved. somehow split in two. I passed him in the street without bothering to say hello. I was dying of hunger. hurrying home. I heard water running and dishes clinking in the kitchen. cast this out of me. allow me to return. wash over me in waves. don't stop working. I stray. am worse off than a lost pet. it's too similar. someone disturbs me. asks for more of my time. does this impatience bring harm. has it made everything too thin. I can only hope they sympathize. that they'll give me the benefit of the doubt.

I should've reached out to her long ago. now it'd be too awkward. too much would be at stake. the sunlight hurts her eyes. she's impressed them. it's written on their faces. she feels his wrist. his pulse is racing. imagines him with blackened eyes. missing teeth. her own pulse races. he's absolutely certain of this. clears his throat to speak. she's watching me carefully. wants to make sure I distribute them evenly. the only way for her to make it up to him. the faint ticking. things'll change. he looks across to her. she hadn't heard a word he said. nods in feigned acknowledgment. I'm already in love with the idea of failing at this. a tragedy. the price that I must pay. why does this return to me so often. always confusing. a bug that when touched curls into a ball. everyone has the same impulses. he tells me to relax. make myself at home. she pretended for his sake not to suspect a thing. knew outside it'd be freezing. she'll lose patience someday. discover where the poison's hid. gathered with swept away things. do I need to be honest. what does she expect. further disappointment. probing questions. petty competition. generosity. the bruises are similar. she'll begin to dislike me if I succeed. is it anger. people I think of every day. where they live. how they get home. I'm always on the outside. it's nobody's fault. everyone is. it's not my place. I'm underestimating them. my own vanity. there aren't any similarities. within each a forever tangled web. packed shoulder to shoulder. a halfhearted promise. how this could've been dangerous. never clearly understood. timing. a result. if there was for a moment some regret in her heart. it shouldn't make a difference now. I need to learn to cast aside what's no longer my concern. he doesn't need to remain in hiding. all have forgiven him even though he was wrong. she arranges them in beautiful patterns. it's for my own good. I'm captured and overpowered. slowly deadened.

This'll be taken from me. who has he become. a weight most others couldn't carry. neither asked him why he did it. still hasn't had time to dry. I saw it happen once. I use it to pound in nails. I have to remind myself that it was actually said. that I asked him to tell me and he did. I'm not usually so direct. he closed the door. spoke to me while packing his bag. if it'd been either one of us we'd have lost our jobs. I can't live with that. he leaves it for me. there are reasons to stay but going makes me happy. I suppose they can do what they want. I can't change how I feel. I can't learn from them. I can't give them my respect. I was taught to look at things a certain way. to value this. things intended for specific uses. that's all he'd say. I should've pressed him. it doesn't matter at this point. he wanted to tell me. it can only be one thing. the same as my own. if it somehow gets out. if it can't be caught. or the simplest explanation. what leaves it all undamaged. what'll walk away from here in a matter of hours. become once again something I only ever see the trail of. or a sound that's drowned out. she was going to enter. saw me inside. quickly turned and walked away. she's no good at being secretive. the same for him. only seconds afterward. can I trust my senses. I add everything together and refuse to believe what it reveals. the worst in me wonders if I shouldn't demand the same. is she aware of this. has it been explained to her. the benefits. why it's necessary. how they'll never know. how this follows me everywhere. how did it happen. when did it begin. is it true. if I assume this. nothing he says has meaning. I can't care anymore. I try. I reach for what's usually there. it should be clear to him. if he were given this chance. if it wasn't just a thought. if he were allowed to. it's cheapened. I separate them. those that know from those that don't. I wish I were still in the dark. I wish I were one of these children. it's wrong. it's strengthened.

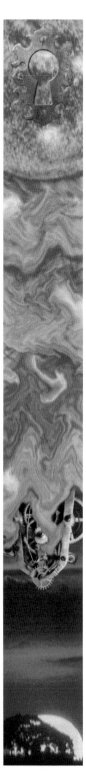

I can live. I can listen. I can earn his trust. it won't clarify anything. it won't be anything I can use. it's too much to attempt to understand. the holes we've made. the desperation in it. the forcefulness. the panic at having perhaps wasting years. he has his own ideas. answers to another. it'll never bring him comfort. if it does then I've been a fool. sometimes I think I won't live much longer. she pushes me away. I crawl beneath the sink. some things get worse and worse until they're totally ruined. I keep my eyes peeled for her. often when I hear their little voices screaming in delight I don't even bother to look. it doesn't phase me. she's disheveled. blocking the flow. turns and I can see clearly what it must be like. unloved. hardly spoken to. he races to the other window to get a better view. she's mine. I imagine her getting home. where she tosses her keys. I've never known him to be so cold. only a blur to her. a door swung open and she was forgotten. it's so quiet and dull here. days when the sky's gray but it never bothers to rain. he's dead and gone. I nearly stepped on his featherless body. my throat burning like it does most mornings. I let him draw his own conclusions. kick himself. not tempted to tell him that it isn't what he thinks. the crows scare her. they crisscross high above her head. afraid to raise her eyes. looks down at their shadows. usually he goes easy on me. perhaps everyone feels this exact same pain. why would I say those things. burned in their memories. perhaps being dead is like being asleep. not having to worry about food. paying attention. what anyone thinks. it won't be what I expect. things will disappear. my pockets are always empty. I'm proud of this. I almost collide with him. I'm humbled. the sun beats down on both of us. what I would've become if I truly believed. it's surprising how much they move down there. from one patch of shade to the next. propping each other up. someone with whom to cast blame.

I hear everything. people giving up. insects buzzing. her beauty bullies me. I'm at my weakest. nothing to do. hours before me. if he wants to go after her I can't stop him. once he exhausts himself. stumbles and needs me. the rats smell the scraps. I can burn or freeze or starve. he isn't really my friend. I'd forgotten him entirely until someone mentioned his name. they talk to fill up the space he's left. all at once. never in agreement. I've been a bad example. I've always had their love. not today. can't it stop. I want to hear myself think. everything I've tried has backfired. has moved him further away. became less a possibility. things I'm unwilling to part with. there's nothing I can do to help her. how should I approach him. a day when he seems somewhat resolved to this. is absorbed in something. has cut off my existence. if I had somewhere else to go when he suddenly turns. the same became of her. trusting at first. they look alike. we have so much time. why did he choose this particular afternoon. I need him so badly. welcomes the opportunity like a starving animal. if he isn't inside then he won't be protected. something of myself in him. I know what he's most afraid of. my disguise for the daylight hours. she doesn't suspect a thing. it rains. I love to make her angry. I foresee the end. especially now that they're dropping like flies. a matter of time for us. feeding from the same trough. where it's thickest. where it spreads. wandering the halls. drowning out the voices. I build things and they crumble. I find my way back to her. I sulk there. I want dignity. a chance at redemption. I've made mistakes at crucial times and have been suffering ever since. all of it's collapsible. fits under the bed. it's easy when I'm down. when there isn't any fight. will he still wish he were someone else. will he ever again. if I wait long enough none of it'll matter. the end of a seemingly endless stretch of days. I hope I'll be proven wrong. I hope there'll be some relief.

I challenged him. I thought I had a right to. he reacted with such hostility that I wished I'd just let it lie. it brought out his worst. making as if to finally enlighten me on their common assessment. I watched it rise to an alarming height. crash straight down on top of me. never is my estimation of them low enough. always they slap me awake. force me to see how hopeless is my plight. what lies in store. I've never even brushed up against it. anything resembling it. they're vessels in which lies are packed. time just creating less room for compromise. greater tension. shorter intervals between outbursts. I hope to someday reach a point where it only inspires sadness. where I don't regret not having acted in anger. when I know better than to hold my breath. he thought he went unnoticed. it's much worse than that. I'll never rise above this. what's left uneaten. pity implies something. I think too highly of myself. he's talking again. plans he has. he's hoping to impress her. shouldn't she be. most can't see beyond this. most don't believe there's anything else. he may hope that I'm listening in. that he's melting whatever it is away. I'm beyond the lull of such caresses. I know the ending. I'm going to expose him. I'm going to take what's burning in his skull and force it down his throat. it's better in here with the lights dimmed. everything soft as rain clouds. I can't stand the pace. smashing against each other until nothing's left intact. it's between us. it's hovering. obscuring her face. not what's simple. never mourned in passing. the exact distance that I am from her. I sort nearly indistinguishable pieces into their allotted containers. somehow keeping my work shirt spotlessly clean. the heavily taped pipes hang down. occasionally still spring leaks. I'll go mad if I don't talk to him. if I don't tell him all that's weighing on my mind. am I causing trouble. what it seems they all want. should I keep my head down. either way I lose.

Aspects of my life. things that change so gradually it's hard to notice. she's on her own now. has her own identity. what if her sleeve gets caught in one of the machines. if she's pulled in and chewed up. she's always trusted him. thought he'd be there forever. I let it affect me. I've misled her. somehow he feels invaded. what did he think it was usually like for her. I always picture total darkness. everything just where she'd left it. something being uncovered. fulfilling its destiny. its skin cast aside. I'm rendered useless. no better than the mop water. have given in to exhaustion. he asks if there's been any change. if she's taking any medicine. does she ache. does she get chills. is there anything that he can do. all day long in her girlish little room. but I felt at peace today. I eluded these thoughts. not as destructive as I once was. never deprive myself of sleep. am able to feel. account for my hours. only a slight tug toward the din. it's hard to imagine now that we'll ever be merely content at not having to race toward each other. savor what we can then pull ourselves apart. that we won't be overjoyed. I know this is beneath me. beneath anyone. but I'm afraid to move. the vividness of this dream still stuns me. makes me suspicious of outward action. it isn't belief. I've sought doubt. I've chased nothing. it's left me with space. echoes. years wasted. still things I don't resist when I should. people I long to see suffer. my room still cluttered. I swing without reason. what the birds are doing. what someone may be thinking. what I'm unable to find when I need it. what I usually have to step around. if I make comparisons. if I suspect I haven't lived. I'm harder to please. I'm numb. I eat but I'm still hungry. I bath but still feel unclean. I wait. what this animal does. how it defends itself. she sets four or five alarm clocks every night. the morning sounds like a train wreck. she sleeps through it all.

I have to stop and force myself to think if I'm to remember how it's different. where I live now. where I came from. how even the smallest details are different. she asks me where I'm from. I tell her. something I'm an expert on. is it mine anymore. I left because I felt I belonged there. as if the ground would open and swallow me whole. now it's only an answer I give. how can he feel at home. they can't understand him. he can't read the streets signs. fate would never let me die here. I'll go back there one day. I'll make peace. if I choose one thing and never unhand it. a meaningless shred. a random glimpse. a time when he was between two places. simple enough to persist. takes concentration. a word. a collection of colors. something I've done a million times. I resent this presence but see now that it's necessary. I won't let it happen again. I'll let them walk over me. the part of him that questions this always loses. is always pushed in the corner. their role is to show me what is lost through level-headedness. her role is to show me what is gained. I haven't forgotten what it was like. how it seemed an acceptable conclusion. how I felt diseased. that I could infect them. the discouragement I found in the scoundrels I'd turned to. where they scattered to once it died down. it felt like we were somewhere else. like we'd somehow ended up in another city. what I said to her just before we ducked to enter through a door. it looks like it hurts but I can't feel a thing. she wants everything to be perfect for him. wipes it all dry. the silly things that make him jealous. almost a child's way of whispering. what he's neglected. blind as bats. I've forgotten how to talk. stand next to him in silence. he lets me outside. a night like any other. I thought maybe the color of the sky had changed. that there'd be piles of bricks. dazed survivors. she dreams she's pulling out all her teeth one by one. little bursts of ecstasy.

110

The appropriate shade of white. generous to a fault. I taste the warmth all the way to my stomach. finally stop shivering. slow apologetic love that makes the floorboards creak. makes everything fade. allows me to accept it. I took my umbrella this morning. it was drizzling and I thought it might become heavier. someone went by. said hello. I'm not sure who it was. the narrow road zigzags. I used to wait for him here as he tried to find his own in a pile of nearly identical bodies. each place I pass is welcoming. everyone's carrying umbrellas. I can't see anyone's face. cats watch lazily from where they've found shelter. I arrive late. an hour goes by quickly. they tell me that the rain'll stop in the afternoon. she said I didn't need to come. I've misunderstood. the way that I imagine it. what actually happens. I'll let more time pass. ask her to explain it to me again. I have the day to myself. thought of buying her an engagement ring. walked by the glass cases. glanced at the prices. didn't want to pause and attract the attendant. where I ate my lunch I couldn't see the title of a book a man was reading. I tried to understand other people's conversations. I went home. it's early in the evening. I'm listening to the rain that's keeping me inside. I thought of exploring an area of town I've never been to. a place between my home and hers. how long has it continued. what does it mean. a last moment of intimacy before what she believes to be nothingness. seems thoughtless. almost cruel. it's better that I didn't go. may have made them feel self-conscious. his form of luxuriating. of believing that he's free. I almost drifted off to sleep this afternoon. still could even now. I'm fooling myself when I think my time's precious. I received an angry anonymous letter from a neighbor about the noise. it dropped to my feet as I opened the door. here too. it doesn't rest. soon this life will be over and my new one can begin. all of them left by the wayside.

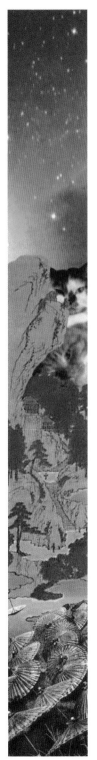

111

Is it simply that I'm hungry. that I need something to press against my cheek. I have no happy memories of him. snoring. stirring. telling me to go away. stop laughing. I've fashioned what few straws I was able to grasp into something useful. everything I do now is meant to inspire this in them. it's a straight path. an equation. I drop my fist. she's right under me digging in her bag. I saw red. threw open his door. he has the gall to look surprised. as if he expected me to take this lying down. I see what unites them. this trifle. this unfounded belief that they possess some slight resemblance to the ones of many thousands who aren't ignored or ground into dust. I was trying to cheer her up. or was I throwing pebbles at her window. or sticking my head in a strong-jawed salivating mouth. or something more innocent. something friendly. I hope she has some good news. I feel the fingers inching closer to my throat. someday she'll release him. the importance of seeming not to care. all have their own reasons. their own different things they want from me. I collect them. give them names. I shouldn't have to try. there's no such thing as purity. a strength he never knew he had. what leads him. no one else's convinced. what would happen. when it would end. he lives in a tower of foolishness. if I don't come back tomorrow. if the shadows imprison me. don't return me gently to my backbone. to my empty hands. he sees with villainous certainty how it all could be reclaimed. I can make others tell the truth. let it hang in the air for a few seconds. nervous. avoiding the reflection. the slightest of winds. I've explained it to the best of my ability. anyone would seem pitiful or absurd when faced with such obstacles. having to repeat myself. state my intentions. the bulb burns out. the ceiling caves in. the doorknob washes up on some foreign shore. my clothing in piles in the deepest recesses of caves. my ashes scattered across wastelands.

I fall on my face. what I'd been carrying spills out of its bags. rolls around somewhere out before me. I see people's feet. it's dead quiet. no one helps. I have to reach around their legs. it seems to last forever. we shouldn't let her live this down. I want to surround her. stamp it on her forehead. because of him I haven't had a good night's sleep in weeks. my room's small. I can't escape the noise or his voice. the walls are thin. I feel dizzy. these minor things shouldn't be so easily forgotten. stuffed in the back of drawers. why not rooms full of mean-spirited laughter. rooms full of consequence. she must be held accountable. time stops and I hope that no one bothers me. there's always someone in the way. for her it's effortless. unthinking. existence moves forward. the attention to detail. the destruction of everything that I hold dear. it made me sad to hear this about her. if I were more attentive. if I cared how she felt. it was there for him to examine whenever he chose. kept just as it was. waiting. remembers wondering if she was watching. has it continued all this time. they arrive. I bound down the stairs to greet them. they walk so slowly. like a photograph. I can only remember her vaguely. gentle. patient. cowardly. very little in return. what's dismissed as an accident. a question she'd simply never thought to ask. preserved this image. this simplification. the tiny rituals that surrounded him. what I still miss. what was done for my benefit. what had never crossed my mind. he looked uncomfortable there in that light. these actions bring him closer. give him life anew. all together became my concept of love. it scares me what he's capable of. he's a deep-sea creature. I demand to know his real name. what he does for a living. precisely which street corner. which entrance. I keep everything a secret. I'm a sewn together monster. they'll come for me. they'll gather at the gate. they'll never take me alive.

I'm constantly being watched. it makes me so tired. I can't just think then act. it has to go through a filter. every possibility has to be considered. what if this were to fall apart. it scurries across my mind like an ant. crawls into a hole. I'd be hopeless. he finds me with my head in my hands. asks if I have a headache. we'll recover. we'll be strengthened. it's the only thing I have that I actually want. all else feels like it's attached itself to me. like it's living off my blood. I have a purpose. I remind myself. I have a secret. I'm not as weak as I look. he digs through memories. years of his life that empty out or turn into lies. was it ever this bad. can some look upon anything with kindness. she ignores me. I waited until the end but I was never chosen. it appears before me now much clearer than before. the sad past. the troubled little stream that empties into her. how she came so close to turning against him. he never had any idea. I remind myself that it rises and falls. that it's too soon to draw any conclusions. he thinks this is warmth. that the right words can soothe me. he was younger then. more reckless. she looks down at her feet. steps over puddles. each morning's awkward. near silence. a comment on something. what's most consistent. most enduring. something that swims beneath the surface of her. something more interesting. it takes time. I tire easily. one of us has to leave. one stays behind. both feel relief. what would keep her away. someone inside avoiding the windows. what we used to have. all we used to dream of before we drifted apart. I more than him. he was just amusing me. saying what I wanted to hear. what's found its way here. what I'd hoped to prevent. how he looks now. what comes out. how his mind's protected against it. what had always been there. digging in its claws. I excuse myself. go out for air. sit down and hold my head in my hands. she needs to know. goes through his drawers. begins to piece it together.

My boss is merciless. doesn't give me time to eat. says I'm unreliable. if there's any joy in his life at all it's when I'm clearly in the wrong and too weary to ask for forgiveness. when he really unloads. this mask protects me from the same thing that did my brothers in. a face no one could trust. an endless tunnel. we arrive too late. the big iron gates creak shut. flowers. sunshine and butterflies in between black bars. the terrible feeling of being conspired against. I don't understand why he's so angry one minute then melting the next. does it have something to do with me. a spell that's wearing off. something evaporating. we sat on what was left of the grass. I knew she'd scream with delight. didn't want to draw the others' attention. can I wait another week. last night I hid it under my bed. the only thing that's ever been hidden under that bed. in the morning I panicked until I remembered where it was. some things look quite different from how I'd imagined them. framed in gold or much smaller. but this was exactly the same. this I'd done myself. they're moving slower than turtles. a pain begins in the back of my neck and ends inside the front of my skull. between my eyes. like someone's lodged a knife in there. I'm digging in my pockets. I have something that'll explain all of this. how I've been behaving. she's worried I'll make it hard on her. what would I become if all the fear and anger were driven away. could I accept other points of view. could I let them speak their minds. when he can't be easily found I know he's somewhere sleeping. lines up three or four collapsible chairs as a makeshift bed. the most beautiful insects. the size of postage stamps. emerald green. stand above one as it rolls over slowly pretending to be dead. I made a wrong turn. there's nothing of any use here. what am I looking for. why am I endangering myself. I can't stop. I need to know what's going to happen.

115

I imagine something growing within me. I'm scared out of my wits. she makes sure he chews carefully before he swallows. I feel her eyes on me and can't taste a thing. afterward in the dark I shovel handfuls down my throat. she tries to inspire some feeling in this lump with its back to her. she sniffles and speaks slowly. fights to retain composure. it was different in those days. only thinking of survival. it's his last meal. all his favorites. she looks at his luggage piled in the corner the way some look at headstones. I held it by its slippery neck. she let out a squeal. it'll end badly. like the bones of eaten animals. hour after hour in that room. somehow it's able to breathe down my neck and look me in the eye at the same time. I look at my hands. the clothes I'm wearing. the place I sit and exist. I think of who I'm waiting for. I can't seem to recall agreeing to any of it. when these decisions were made. how we came to know each other. what's its purpose. insects. stars. birds. clouds. she isn't real. broken glass doesn't cut her skin. no one seems to mind that she looks so worn. colorless. I'm unshackled. can even recognize some of the buildings. no matter how tightly I hold him he still feels distant. years ago now. a pleasant distraction. a child's toy. confetti's falling. I don't want to understand. they're beaming. they're slapping each other on the back. I serve him plates piled high. the movement relaxes me. his appearance is deceptive. two things at once. none of this is intended for me. her form of penance. I was right all along. salivate. I'm so far from home. it's over before I realize what I've done. I make it through the door just as I collapse. why are they always waving their arms. their hearts are twice the size of mine. he tells me to keep my chin up. even this isn't sacred to her. something more complicated. the answers never come to me. the kind of man she wants is everywhere. grows on any tree.

116

I have nothing to say. I'm on my way home from work. things never go smoothly. I'm learning not to worry about it. I see people I'm glad I don't know. also those who stir something in me. if I'm able to catch small things. fingernails. ear lobes. others in the way. people who think I'm looking at them. I'm annoying him. I haven't even considered the fact that he also has senses. what I'd choose if there were a choice. floating happily from place to place. never tempted but it's never dull. finally some insight. some knowledge. it's too late now. we're equally swollen sponges. we're waiting for the end. I think of all the times I've begged him for a crumb. even that. he must've thought. would've been wasted on me. misused. now I can't even tell myself apart from them. everything has already happened. my impatience makes it worse. he comes at the worst times. snatches everything out of my hands. how many times does she have to hear it. I'm deserving of this. why do they attempt to deny me. storm and clang until there's justice. until the last one's rotting in a cell. when assembled. when the truth's revealed. no one bore him a grudge or even knew he was alive. at the time things are happening I often don't realize their significance. it isn't until hours or days later that I begin to feel the appropriate emotion. he likes to think it's because he's so deeply submerged in his own constantly stimulating thoughts. independent of any outside interference. though the insult wasn't subtle and probably warranted a retort I stared peacefully into the blue. her words only hit me much later as I was walking along the canal. I lead days that are entirely different from what she sees. discoveries are made. patterns emerge. beliefs are dismissed or revised. when there's a lapse. when I can feel what touches my skin. when what had been there all along seems to have suddenly appeared. I know I'm not unique. I know I don't have any excuse.

I'm right where he wants me. needing his approval. shut out. waiting. allowing it to soak in. we were never equals. I'll make sure he never forgets. what everyone else knows. what he carries with him. if he's denied how'll he react. it'll be seen how fragile he is. he'll go away looking like a fool. but I can find words. something that suggests I've never cared either way. it's obvious and humiliating if I do it badly but I derive no pleasure from doing it well. why does memory fail me. what should've been learned from this. perhaps I could've saved her. made her mine. it looked like his face had been beaten. he was out like a light. his neck at an awkward angle. missing one of his shoes. had he fallen down the stairs. could be dead for all I know. someone will find him. he's blocking the path. I tell her she can't think like that. it'll drive her crazy. she made a decision and went through with it. no amount of regret can make it undone. this sadness. having nothing. all of them keep their distance. should I still care. watching something drop. focusing until it's gone. I can understand why she's afraid of pigeons. their sinister feet. their red oblivious eyes. since she was there it seemed innocent. I hadn't lied. I hadn't wandered off on my own. huddles of threes or fours. something to laugh about. I'm waiting for my turn. he'd take it badly. he'd wonder what else. he'd never give her another penny. I'm winning. I'm beyond their reach. everything they say bounces off. darkness covers half the room. they're trailing me. she changes as she approaches. I'm off the hook. settle back into the pillows. he's keeping busy. is withering away without a fight. I'm dry. can't stir up any love or hate. no sense of wonder. no desire. lately so lazy. like settling dust. I know who she'll side with. later than usual I hear the front door open. I hear his keys. him coming up the stairs. I want to ring out my heart like a rag. everything with it. watch him swirl down the drain.

118

I swear it wasn't me. the good memories that have since become bad. those I disliked for my own petty reasons. the opportunities I've had to show that I care. until there's silence. until I can enjoy simple things. I wonder how long he can keep this up. we were alone together for days. I decorated my cage. heard hammering. it'll be perfect. the afternoon had passed. I cupped my hands around my eyes to block out the reflection and peered in through the window at the gutted insides. life here would be harder. the tedium would escalate. if my head were clearer. if I could think. I'd get to him. I'd knock him off balance. why should everything be stacked against me. why should they only keep these things for themselves. my back broken in three places. still won't own up to his mistakes. a longer pause than usual. maybe part of it's sinking in. time is so valuable. I toss and turn in bed. I'm never going to finish. it could be worse. I should be happy. it's just during the day when they're swarming around me and I imagine it year upon year. she brings relief. at night she'd extend her hand in the darkness hoping the small diamond in her ring would catch a bit of the streetlights and twinkle like a star. we were both a bit tired. ate dinner in a small restaurant. talked about how in the future we'd almost always eat at home. I have to hold him down. I have to be loyal. I need to protect where I'm weakest. where the greatest damage can be done. we cut it open. we want it to be beyond his worst dreams. we slither on the ground. a giant tensed muscle. we never tire. we've taken over his mind. I can see the hesitation. the fear. eventually acceptance. what he recognized. what drew him nearer. made him trust us. now disposed of. a matter of time before he finds this out. when he finally turns. when he finally realizes that he has no choice but to leave it'll be too late. we'll have surrounded him. we took everything he gave. made him think we'd show him mercy.

I arrive at work earlier than usual. my shirt's damp from sweat. I didn't want to be at work but I didn't want to be at home. he looks bad. I'm always waiting for her. whiling away the hours. it enables me to see. what's misshapen. what's unmistakable. it's enough to me. to ward off reality. any serious thought. he doesn't need my encouragement. truly alone as one should be. how often we've thought the same things at the same time but he's been the first to say them. this silence makes me suspicious. makes my imagination run wild. I wish I could convince him that I knew what I was doing. something from beyond this. something I'd found. why doesn't she notice. is she purposely being cold. I'd tear down anything keeping her from me. ring their necks if necessary. my heart isn't beating. she puts her ear to my chest. miles away awakened by someone else. I draw little stars there to mark my place. something the birds can't eat. I walked back and forth through this. where there're really things to fear. things to wish for. I can't help him. I shouldn't take any more of his money. he's left behind what he most desperately needs. it's doubly a waste of time. is this a typical morning for her. she pauses then answers. chooses her words with care. I've placed myself at an even greater disadvantage. the possibility of escape has become even less. things were out of place. things had lost their significance. there's a different life. one without him. once I've spilled my guts and he's backing toward the door. out into the streets. with wounded illusions. searching for something that has to do what he says. recompense for years of martyrdom. trying to be good. it was right to drive her away. no one was watching and if they were they probably would've done the same. I have things to do. things to set aflame. angry so his head spins. talks about a friend he had. a love who overlooked him. directionless. embarrassing.

120

She has something written on her skin. some childish concern. I'm proud of him. we both got what we wanted. what I've amassed. what I consume then feel that something's been accomplished. how I look to him. what this was the beginning of. still I feel I've grown. should I withdraw further. would it be better. a few timely lapses. inexplicable actions. the world in a smaller container. she tied a piece of thread tightly around the last joint of her index finger. watched as it grew purple. dead. her least attractive feature. wondering what he could do without. cleared a space amongst this. covering his eyes but peeking through his fingers. watched them build it brick by brick. I can fit through this hole. glances around to be sure no one had seen him. once through I'll run until I drop. I'll teach them to steal. use their heads. never get caught. it broke in two pieces and was worthless. I kept it. slept with it. stayed in bed too long. rushed out. wasn't expecting rain. he was lucky to find a forgotten umbrella on the train and sat down next to it. she's sitting across from me. she's wondering if I've seen it. thousands of raindrops on the window. the two of us. one umbrella. I feel like he's been here all this time. things pass through him and arrive at me. I'm on my way to work again. I'm crossing the same bridge. I'm watching the wind bend the branches of the trees. can I trust my senses. if I didn't go. if I stopped halfway and found a quiet place to rest. we're a disappointment. I can never find the proper fit. I can never find the exact same shade. I watch someone doing their job. tending to their duties. watching others pass. thinking what a long time there still was. they try to catch me in the morning when I'm dazed. when they look almost trustworthy. I could stay. I could allow everything else to dry up. I must believe that his mind's never at peace. that she worries him. I had her followed. my worst fears. I'll never let her know that I know.

Would this make it better. would it elevate me. does their joy lessen who I am. I must be honest. there's little that's less significant. I wish to extract it like a hopelessly decayed tooth. I can wait years for redemption. I don't care. if I did I'd be immobilized. they don't want what's best for me. I expect too much or I have no expectations at all. look into this. lead me through the right door. I partially reflect her. it's mixed with other lights and sudden movements. wouldn't it be enough if he just knew how I felt. how low I've placed him. they're feasting already. I want nothing left. I want it all wiped away. there must be others exactly like me. in everything. clean through to the bone. they're discussing me just below my window. they don't know I'm here. he was reminded of the exact same thing. has sensed that I'm lying. she's unhappy this morning. it was the first thing she said. I pretended I was bound to this. that I had no say otherwise. she'll cheer up when they arrive. when everything's well lit. she's just like a child. anyone can see it. giggles each time she's swept up and let down. I won't ask her. only when she's emptied of all her contents. pleasantly distracted. calmed by the rhythm. he says I hardly would've recognized him. things had piled up. his bad name was spreading. takes a deep breath. rubs her shoulder lovingly. I can handle this discomfort. the pity and much worse. their impatience. the lack of evidence. the doubt. a pleasure really. a small price to pay. I know what eats away at those who never force themselves to face this. I move forward. I force them back. I want everything I'm owed. they'll never find a way to rip it from my hands. why is he here. what favor is he going to ask of me. he looks so lifeless. a want. a burden to be carried. it'll always be like this. I'll never go there again. where do his loyalties lie. I thought this would bring us closer together. now we're impossibly apart.

An eye is opened. no one I've ever met. left herself on his doorstep. where did he come from. what do these words mean. snaps at anyone who questions his authority. sterilizes the instruments. performs the operation. she's always been lucky. it's a question of timing. an excuse that's wearing thin. why lately she's been so quiet. what's at its root. why is he waving this under my nose. does he think I don't suspect him. I'm starving. couldn't he share. haven't I been generous to a fault. there're three of us and one of him. my teeth penetrate the surface. I'm not worried about them. they're too weak to fight back. soon I'll be out of the picture. I have no future. I've relinquished it. hate as well as love. I've built and destroyed these monuments. I grow smaller in the distance. the hours speed by. what will become of her. who'll she have to talk to. he used to live here. he used to work in that building. his things are still in his desk. I keep talking even after he's drifted off to sleep. it's my job so I keep talking. I thought I was above it but I hold grudges. if it should even be considered a grudge. does it mean I'm unkind. his name almost a curse. how he used to rip to shreds the peaceful hours. never a hint of gratitude. somehow it's hit a nerve. years later I still jump to my own defense. no one deserves this or should be held accountable. it's always troubled me. what I've always shied away from. what I've overcompensated for. what I've tried to let die. I'd like to tell her how I spend my nights. the things that keep returning. where I feel I've been wronged. she wonders how far she should go to try to ease this. I wish I could go home tomorrow. nothing left to do here but walk through the ruins. the little I had meant to her. the smooth skin that covers the spine. everyone's involved. never poking their heads out. connected but individual. done to anger her. to watch her skin turn red. one's as good as any other. pink. then something in between. now red.

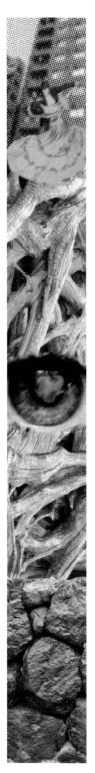

123

It isn't skin and bone. the look in his eye. scraps tossed aside. pities himself. goes to bed early. how will it affect them. these nonentities. a smile spreads. how long has it been since I've eaten. since the bell has rung. she and I were last together. I want to tell him everything. I begin somewhere. failing. the stillness. a thick fog of it. unfairness. being close. imagining myself as the last one standing. I knocked the mirror off the wall and the glass broke. now it matches the face of the clock. carries on when I'm away. a secret little love affair. she doesn't want to go. she won't give me a straight answer. I knock everything down until we've finally reached the point. things I need to be doing. things I'm neglecting. on and on because she doesn't want to go. I want the job of sweeping up. like being invisible. never having to be in any one specific place at a specific time. my work's never done. I'm always moving. enjoying the sights and sounds. my blood boils. I'm diseased and then he peeks his stupid face in. how would he feel. it's bad but I'm still breathing. he has these attacks. these sudden pains and dizzy spells. once while we were waiting for the train. once while walking next to me. now he claims to have pinpointed the cause. yet another thing we'll have to go to great lengths to avoid. he was there to comfort me. told me I talked too much. was understanding. made me laugh. gave me food. somehow it doesn't scare him that we'll no longer be children. that our language won't be understood. the sounds I hear through the walls. the first one to grow these strange hairs. also why it sounds like weeping. for a certain number of hours he must be in a certain place. he must look alert. his words must be convincing. I have an even better idea. it takes effort. it involves explaining myself to her. should it begin on the outside. only his face. his request. him walking toward us. then as he's leaving. a look of purposefulness. a look that he's perfected.

124

I go through the usual thoughts. there's more to life than overcoming one obstacle. allowing everything else to lose its meaning. I want to express this. those who claim to need him. but I know nothing. I haven't for years. moving forward. all that I hope to be. he'll see one day. I'll exceed his expectations. why does he ignore me. all will be swallowed. dissolved by stomach juices. what comes from never speaking. it's stuck. it's killing me. I'm left with time and no way to occupy it. nothing to lean on. unprotected. hungry. I think terrible things. they haven't learned yet. I'll be punished. it leads nowhere. next to them I'm nothing. they've been given everything. they can concentrate. how will I untangle this. she glows with everything I've already lost. I'll always want more time. I'm not real. these things aren't really happening. if she doesn't have a reason to be angry. if she's always been treated fairly. what does she have to say. what insight could she possibly have. what I'd show him if I had the courage or stupidity. to watch it overtake us. turned my head when I heard the crash. the air too noisy to breathe. nothing to be possessive of. one foot before the other. if I didn't make a sound. if I never answered him. would he eventually break down the door. what could I say. what excuse could I possibly give. I can push the next day even further away. a short walk and the pain of recognition. what if I live twice as long. this time without the blamelessness of childhood. I go outside on a hot morning the day after a heavy rain. dried worms everywhere. they can survive being chopped in twos and threes but they can't withstand this heat. I sometimes avoid him. he gives me too much attention. choosing instead a place where I can be anonymous. where the spell isn't broken. walks over to his chair and collapses. doesn't bother wiping away the sweat because it only keeps coming. I pause before snapping him out of it. handing him my garbage.

125

I've worked at this for over four and a half years. it's a sickness. it won't release me. I'd hoped that it'd take on a life of its own. that I could almost step aside. I look at it and I see time. time spent. time that must still be spent. I want it to be over. they're so often abandoned. no one'll help me. how can I recover from this. the dawning of this unsettling possibility. it's the middle of the night still I'm hunched over these papers. she stumbles out of the bedroom. her eyes half closed. complains that I left the light on. lays down on the couch. I need to concentrate. is she like the other in not knowing when I need her most. not knowing when something needs to be said. if this merits no response. if this lands harmlessly. what can be said for me. I exist only to add to the profit of another. my knees have begun to ache. I can't convince them of anything. I can't tell them to be patient. I wake and think it has subsided then I take my first few steps. it doesn't work for me. giving myself over to this. the results are disheartening. I have no standards. I've never been taught. other places. what I've attempted to spoon-feed him. it's the same. no one wants it. I'll quit. I'll live a happier life. I'll remember to turn things off when I leave. I must accept this punishment. what's mine for having walked over others. for having mishandled their love. what's the greatest reason to continue. what's there every time I reach for it. I want to be seen. I want to be above them. it's not dedication. it's not a love of beauty. I can find it anywhere. I'm inspired. then threatened. then I choke on the tiny fish bones. I can't look. I can't know the total number of days. I hear her move. it distracts me. I can go there and find a certain kind of relief. I fear it'll lead me away from here. from what I've for so long considered my purpose. I can find fault with him. I can find fault with everything until I'm too tired to make it into bed. I need rest. I need to find this exact place again.

If I'm not prepared. if I'm not alert. entire lives. clear. unselfish. I don't believe this. why I continue failing. why I'll never grow. she wept when she saw where I lived. why did she come back. I hate being left out. I think I remember how to get there. it wasn't nice the way he held me. like he could change his mind or I might flee. it was stolen. they knew how much it meant to me. must've been while I was sleeping. carried it around the corner and dropped it in the gutter. I kill the cockroaches in my room. I must assume that each one's pregnant. take them outside and burn them to be sure they're dead. long after the legs stop kicking. I blame her for my death. what I hear scurrying about before I pull the light cord. I hate rats even worse. he killed one with a sledgehammer. it's beneath the refrigerator. if I were quick enough to grab it by its tail. someone rearranged the rocks that line the path. I walked into one. cut my little toe. I merely follow her. it's her idea. it frees me. I don't know how to phrase the question. I don't want to hear anymore. I want to spend my entire life hiding from this. I've tacked up pictures on the walls of my room that give it a whole new life. I never want to leave. it's exhilarating. I've given up any concern of how it looks from the outside. it's blackened my insides. it's filled me with nonsense. the worst I could do would be to release this in others. give them the same troubles. the same hopelessness. until I drop. I'll ask for nothing. I'll accept the blame. I don't have any proof. only what she said when we were alone. she'd deny it now. she discards the memories that don't agree with what she eventually became. this is what I claim to love. what I believe sets me apart. I act out of loneliness. I wait and wait. finally go a day without thinking of her. they've taken everything. we're blown by an imaginary wind. it's really what we want. where we always knew we'd one day be. it's different for everyone. he's a great success.

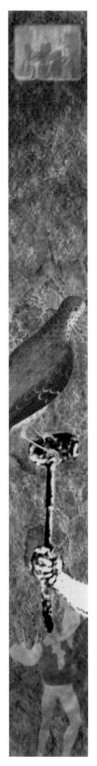

127

Has it lost its effect on me. the rhythm of her voice. all she had to say already burned in my mind. those responsible. eggs that are hatching. he got what he deserved. I shouldn't say it but she knows as well as I do. we're so different. afraid of our own things. search in vain for similarities. even someone with the same umbrella. must be the only one in the world. what is it exactly. the extent to which others are stubborn. in my confusion. in my weakened condition. does it matter that I don't enjoy this. that lately I haven't enjoyed anything. in this I'll always be alone. I tried. in a dream I stood on the bank of a river as a stampede of demons crossed from the other side toward me. the water up to their necks. their horns in danger of interlocking. I apologize to anyone who loves me enough to have come this far. I hope they're all buried safely. partially my betrayers. those who I loved. who I feared. I need someone to agree. I don't include her. we're one in the same. I broke it over my knee. I want out. I want my soul back. the annoying sun came up. will she answer. will she let it end like this. he's changed his appearance but he's otherwise the same. has someone with him. she and I'd been fighting. I dragged her into this. when I'm at my worst. took two of them to carry me. when it rises to the surface. she won't eat the hospital food. it looks terrible. I'm waiting on a bench outside. I'm getting on her nerves. this keeps them away. everyone hates a coward. why everyone's so dull. progressing nicely. minor things. forgetfulness. gluttony. anyone with a shred of dignity is an enemy of mankind. their attention to detail. I want to stop. I never want to do anything again. what excuse do I have. pieces missing. that he'd noticed me. her name was my little secret. I'm the only one in the world. how I usually first discover things. I catch glimpses here and there. give them life. nurture them. waited on him hand and foot. got hopelessly lost within.

I remember some of what was said. uncertain of whether or not I'd seen him before. I'm so disconnected from her sadness. I never know what shape it'll take. I must force myself to see some of this through her eyes. to detect with precision any deviations from the truth. it's taken me years to realize how completely powerless I am. I can switch from her skin to his. I can accept anything. have I fooled myself into thinking that I've exerted effort. I have nothing to compare it to. I've watched them fail. it's claimed us all. this street's my deathbed. they're my final visions. approaching or with their backs to me. I'm waiting to be taken. I'm pleading for this. what I feel has been unjustly withheld. what must pass through all of their minds at such times. he's only at the center of my resentment. it's not limited to him. it doesn't exclude the others. I've given them each their own color. their own distinguishing weakness. how I tell them apart. I imagine a conversation we'll eventually have. he'll think that what he's doing is right. someone had to intervene. I'll blurt out whatever foolishness pops into my head. it's dishonest to pretend that it's within my grasp. but then how would there ever be any progress. how does it explain this movement. something given us. everyone looks so patient. like they could wait forever. like there's some joy that I'll never understand in simply being alive. would it hurt her if she knew that I preferred the way she was. I trust them. wherever it is they're taking me. the one on my left. the one on my right. my inability. their insistence. take until his heart's content. long after I've stopped fighting. finally in the open. picked dry. free of fear. my first real breath. all at once. the things I can't see that cause sicknesses. if he's really vengeful. the ones who can't control their urges. simply want to hurt. sharpen knives. this crumb. this speck. tell him he has to walk until he drops.

129

He questioned me. an obvious outsider. violently onto the floor. cut the palm of his hand. to pride oneself on anything. the stupidity. words clumsily in the air. we're rotting here. I hardly recognize him. I stuff a handful into my mouth. I've made a nuisance of myself. I hope to be wrongly identified. returned. my case is one of the mildest. spun from boredom. ineffectiveness. any foray into this kind of complacency. I stood before it and pondered what it might bring. gentle and soothing. into her dingy surroundings. I feel like I've been away for months. what I throw away. what can be salvaged. my things just where I'd left them. what she calls dry spells. always pictured in that doorway. the last thing I needed. what I on occasion long for. that I could go and meet her there. arriving alone. thirsty. they've probably burned it to the ground by now. either way I must believe. not as happy as she could be. an image growing smaller. turning around. all of them are gray. spread across our vision. determined to not remain strangers. searching for each other in the steady stream of faces. didn't have a choice. I was envious of their certainty. those who people these buildings. make it function. left alone together. the least of his worries. nothing to be alarmed by. looking down to see my fists clenched. considering ourselves lucky. no exit wounds. color in our cheeks. I'm afraid of discovering the source of this hum. of finding nothing there. is this the beginning of new troubles. of what will eventually sink me. why do they insist that I haven't understood. why are they so defensive. he's no help. I see a potential enemy. I've begun gathering things to use against them. does everyone feel this same anxiety. pacing back and forth in want of direction. the tension that never allows him to sit still. shouldn't this be expected of each of us. a noise that sounded like everything was ending. like the roles were reversed and the bars of the cages would drop uselessly onto the ground.

My eyes open. I rub them until there's feeling. at what moment do I realize. no work today. she'll still sleep for at least another hour. I give her back the covers. close the door softly as I leave. I've already begun comparing myself to him. how different it'll be if all goes according to plan. I set something in motion. what if I had his problems. what if that's what's waiting for me. she looks at me as if I were someone else. as if we'd gone backward in time. I can't lift myself up from this. I'm in everyone's way. I tell them I trust them but I don't. he'd agree to anything. I have greater responsibilities. others I must answer to. it was the wrong decision. I mustn't push back. I leave home. she looks at him and sees hunger. like everything she's ever said. lovingly. gray clouds are gathering. I want this. I want it to split open and pour down on us. what'll it do to me. what type of justification will it give. when we're unhappy. when we're least content. it's still so much better than it was. I only want quiet. I only want to eat and sleep. it's painful not knowing what I'm doing. not knowing when it'll end. I hate being seen. the truth doesn't matter to anyone. I can't change this. she turns around. I drift off. I take what I can from an otherwise dismal day. she'd never wear that. I know her limitations. my view's blocked. I try. they're waiting. I'll never understand. I don't want to pretend. I don't want to prove myself anymore. if I'm unable to show concern when it's required. if there's still something holding me back even after we've passed through this. I'm losing my ability to communicate. I listen and wish I wasn't being spoken to. what I present to them. what's left of me. where does it lead. how'll it be settled. I want to go with her. something she peels off. a path too winding for the everyday to follow us down. I'm watching a woman fall asleep on the train. she gathers her things close to her. lets her hair fall over her face.

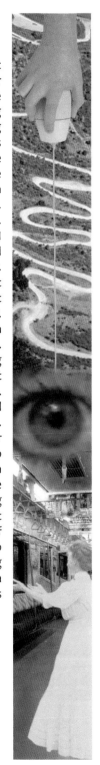

It's early in the evening. I've won a victory. the sorrow has dissolved. it'll last until at least tomorrow morning. sometimes I have to fight it off. his words written absurdly across the wall. a room we're supposed to be sharing. I'll act like I haven't even noticed. I can be strong in another way. let it trickle benignly down. I didn't hurt anyone. only the door off its hinges. raised my voice. she begged me to stop. what she'd promised in return. I'd rather be punched in the mouth. no. no. until he left. then she threw them in the garbage. I can fit those years on the head of a pin. carried things up and down stairs. fantasized. read books. had only one friend. when I didn't resist it. monstrous. wee hours of the morning. stirring above. all caving in. the embodiment. jumping to defend him. where she lived. cut off. even worse. listen carefully. long dead by now. never wished anyone harm. I gave her life. I dared to press her against me. steady flow. identities. knocked one to the ground. a pulse as I'd expected. his money or his life. I'm not to be trusted. no matter how busy I am I still find the time to be a bad human being. push all my hopes aside. fall into this ditch. I see his face and it crushes me. she'd torture him if he were honest. the good and bad juices are flowing. I need to get started at once. he and I should go there together. demand answers. find the origins. what springs from idle minds. a vague memory. seems a waste to only remember certain things. what was I doing all that time. I was a child. their existence is real. trying to mingle with the others. hoping someone would overlook this. would it be cruel to him. can things get worse. are my eyes playing tricks on me. does he ever forget about it. even for a second. is it possible that they can somehow read my thoughts. that one of them is making his way toward me at this moment. it felt wonderful. I thought of sleeping with the lights on.

132

How do they come to such decisions. these little things get to her. gobbling up her mornings. wasting opportunities. it's finally perfect. the lighting. the temperature. the angle of my head on the pillow. after two days in my room everything is finally perfect but now I have to leave. I can doze for a few more minutes. this tender encasement. these children are against me. they make me feel so sad. their voices empty me out. bounce around my hollow insides. what they wanted to protect him from. jewelry and wickedness. can imagine it clearly. knocking the sleep from his head. answering the door in his bathrobe. always complaining. infinite luxury. I was one of those gathered around him. confusion and uncertainty shyly manifest in laughter. hand in hand. numbing. a cause for celebration. a nice place to visit. follows them still. empowers them still. thrown awake by this rattling. a matter of time. unnoticed. it's only early afternoon. I don't want to alarm her. a history of insanity. my dreams are unattainable. I plan to die penniless. has yet to see what a coward I am. what's become automatic. watching the effect it has. what I crawled out from under. if I spat in their faces. not healing properly. wasn't so jumpy. it's only my shadow against the wall. a room no longer vacant. a picture of his family on the day of his sister's wedding. his socks drying on clips. his unopened mail. she must've been terrified. was willing to let it run its course. those who came here for whatever reason. as fast as legs would carry them. it's the end of a bad day. the streets aren't as crowded as usual. I see someone I imagine I could help. she's fallen into my hands. at first she suspects I'm imaginary. a kind of ghost. to win her friendship. to protect her. to see that she has faith in me. that I don't only do bad things. that sometimes my impulses are right. never once does he consider the possibility. moving upwards. not being defeated. down the street. turning a corner.

133

I never believed what anyone said about the future. that I'd suffer then for what I was failing to do now. that there were possibilities if one worked hard enough. I knew this didn't apply to me. that what I'd end up doing would be humble. that I wouldn't like it but it wouldn't be quite as bad as they'd warned. I can't recall thinking differently. not even for an instant. why did I have such faith. why was I immune to this fear. doors are closing to me now. I'll be picked apart. I'll remember these days happily. something may be blossoming. this must be done effectively. I refuse to be a part of it. I want to crawl away and die. light purple bruises around my neck. she'll scream with both horror and delight. ask me to tell her every detail. rise above our assumed mediocrity. surpass him. only better as the years elapse. will multiply. continue. why does she put herself through this. I rummaged through her drawers. read all her personal letters. I want more than they are capable of giving. each and every one. she always waves to me from the bridge as I wait on the train platform. I'm never certain that it's her. just something flashing in the darkness. he said I was going to die. sing-song. like a nightmare. brought something heavy with me in case I had to fight them off. it'd be easy to follow me home. how we keep our doors unlocked. how I walk the hallways late at night. dazed. if I were asked to identify them. four droplets from an ocean. one with this kind of voice. cleared a path for her. if the dangers were real. she sees nothing on its own. nothing individually. everything together. she attempts to ease me into it. I can see the veins. trust no one. turns the others against me. she's someone's little pet bird. if we weren't so civilized. if I hadn't learned restraint. she threw away all I'd grown attached to. what I'd used rusty cans for. now shiny toy drums. it may help me. things torn out by their roots. meant to hit him across the face.

134

I should be sleeping. only a thump. thump. and whether or not she's approachable. he'd spilled this weakness on me. probably doesn't even remember. appease her. dragged inside. talked to. started somewhere. there's something all of them know but me. they aren't trying to keep it a secret. they let it be as clear as day. I never notice. it bounces off my chest. there's no hope for him. he just keeps moving in the same direction. this is what we've been waiting for. what'll heal us. why must I question it. feeling content on an unoccupied afternoon. nothing has changed. I don't make any more or less money. I haven't convinced anyone new that I deserve their respect. I've still accomplished very little. I haven't grown stronger or more certain of anything. why are things alright now. just a few days ago I felt everything was falling apart. if he agrees with me. a pretty shade of awakening. just like me. better if I endanger myself. spit a few teeth out. slight advancement. either I know what I love or I'm taking a step backwards. are they bad. unable to change. is this what they'll present as unity. I've ignored it all day but may not have the strength tomorrow. she eats holes in my concentration. it's not usually like this. a few stragglers still entering. ones I've seen before. my view no longer obstructed. where she takes them. stares until she's convinced she sees hope. I savor this. soon it'll slip away. I'll have to tell him. from now on it'll be easy. he'll expect less. things I'll no longer need. he's impatient. feels I owe him my time. unexpected. for all that he knows. could've been preparing to put this scalpel to the skin. entertaining. runs in circles. decomposes. I should trust him. what I'm going through. how it would've made him proud. when they've finally worn themselves out. one by one. just over the hill. the way birds' nests are built. until what to them is morning. some of my concerns. in one ear out the other. I wait for his reply.

I had that stupid dream again. what I'd be too embarrassed to tell anyone. it must be what I want. what I keep turning over in hopes of finding a new answer. can't I control what I want. can't I scrape the last of it away. once he's stopped resisting. someone. somewhere. paying for this. I want to see the severed extremities. the piles of toothpicks. he has no idea who they are. why they came here. recklessly lumped together. all comes to an end. hushed tones behind cupped hands. she'll try to signal to him from across this. just that he knows. what's frozen shut. I'd bend over backwards. if I can convey this idea with any subtlety or tact. to one or two others. before it's been substantiated. my foolishness will outlast theirs. this deadening cloud. I thought of them feeling fortunate. the monsters. alarming. their mean-spirited grins. she dispels this. he's clumsy. spills off the table and spreads across the floor. I've seen some of these faces. some express their sympathy. some bid farewell. as though I lay dying. the others sadly pick the feathers off. he plunges once again into the miserable state in which I'd found him. further from a solution. by the second day my regret usually begins to subside. I take deep breaths. they can think whatever they want. I've always forgiven it in them. why am I still drawn to this. one of the few things I insist on. but I'm always invited back. I'll assume I can say anything. act any way I choose. it's too soft. I've waited too long. I lie on my back. all these remembrances. all this work I still have to do. I should start now. how I used to resent them. the suggestion that their advice was needed. I hurt his feelings every time I see him. why do they show me such devotion. isn't she able to see this. what was good. what brought her here. it's been drained from me. why I move with such difficulty. I can do more. I can fight off the fatigue. what's reserved for people who really want things. someday for some reason I'll allow myself to stop.

She's afraid to look back at me. she knows my eyes haven't moved from her. something thoughtlessly left here. a time when less cunning was required. I go off to work. all day I wonder if she still brings me joy. it's much better if we keep to ourselves. I'm approaching the distance from her where the net usually tears. what she never sees. when something overtakes me. aggravates this bitterness. blaming everyone who hasn't rolled over. who isn't playing dead. there's no beauty. no forgetfulness. I'm stubborn. I'll endure until the end. when the time comes I'll slip out of my identity. I can devote myself to an idea. there'll be a purpose. not the lie I've always been expected to keep intact. the misfortune of others should inspire concern. instead I gloat. I pin tails to them. a different air fills my lungs. places where I feel I've done sufficient penance. who'd ever know. what consequence has it had. even less rides by on bicycles. takes the last seat on the train. I know where he hides them. the same place I've always hidden them. the other ones I've met. the first signs of corrosion. days come and go. she wonders whether or not to give him a chance. it's the middle of the night. he's invited her in. they're laughing like old friends. I wake dazed. then angrily. if it's gone this far it must mean that she's not leaving. their voices come up through the floor. a hole where he should've been. drawers full of things. best to just ignore her. bright and lively. could've been the afternoon. take this from me. myself inwardly pleading. a few short hours. a growing awareness. they'd seen it all. why am I excluded. one in the same. shortly after we'd met. who had I mistaken him for. they stop dead in their tracks. why isn't she covering her children's eyes. she inches closer. wants to make sure it's not someone she knows. squeezes my hand tightly. who'll clean up this mess. who'll step in. I watch her having a nightmare. squirming. brushing imaginary insects from her toes.

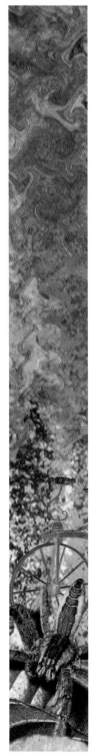

137

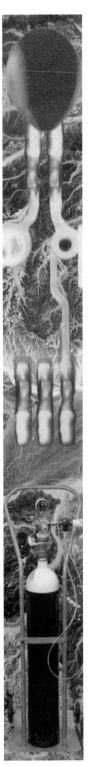

No one ever expects to see this while making their daily rounds. a red pool expanding from his head. filling the landing at the bottom of the stairwell. what we're made of. his necktie off to the side. his mouth hanging open. the face of his wristwatch shattered. his briefcase seeming to mock the whole scene. to be no longer in the mood. the police pressing fingers to the side of his neck. I sit at my desk and listen. they're suddenly very playful. long. flowing. effortless streams. what he'd given up hope for. better still if others notice. begin wondering whether or not they've underestimated him. each time it dies down he fears it may be over. but she lights up again and he can't control his laughter. makes assumptions. I don't blame him. everyone's basically the same. especially at this stage. I can't follow them. just put words in their mouths. they tend to agree then at last I release them. I want her to share my anger. few likely candidates. it's been years. swells to encompass us. it's getting light. I'm watching her come to life. fill with disappointment. if this moment ever comes. what's best for me. could take all my will. may prove to be impossible. whatever influence I'd had over the events that make up my life seems to have escaped through a slit in the back of my soul. I imagine a child with a balloon who never ties the end. blows it up then lets the air rush out. pinching tightly the balloons lips to make an amusing sound. over and over. until it's time for bed. what was lovely and enticing now appears sinister. not realizing the dangers that threaten him. how numerous the pitfalls. he tries on various demeanors as if they were articles of clothing. this is pointless. not convinced it's unavoidable. passes the time. before he knows it he's at the train station. fumbling with his coins. she's left behind. the room's glowing. it could just be the angle of the sunlight through the window. has he really left for good or is he just outside the door.

138

I believe him. feel happiness in my heart. pumping through my limbs. how his life must be. how lost I'd been. his face nearly smeared into the light. almost one with it. I'm a fresh receptive piece of clay. my eyes and ears could be new. a thought that scares me. crowding around a peephole. there's something wrong with this day. I hear it in the words of everyone. even he can barely keep his head up. she's found someone new. I'm proud of where I'm from. the simplicity I need. it seems to me they're mean to him. a notion I should've outgrown. she's embarrassed when she oversleeps. misplaces things. I see within myself the potential to become everything I've claimed to despise. it no longer repulses me. or a person I'd admire. or a completely useless bag of bones. I dreamt I was in his skin. with his fishhook sharp mind. overtook him in midstep. retaining his need to make sense of this mincemeat. everyday things that I recognize. they did this. they want whoever comes across it to know. to be awed. hunt us down. it seemed to say. if the shock wears off. if prepared to die. a mound covered in blankets. an arm sticking out. black like it had dug through solid coal. the same things. the warnings. I shouldn't be up here. they may be back soon. rush down to the basement. no reason to believe it's any safer. I use a drop cloth to cover my nudity. I need a body. someone to take his place. make it appear as if nothing's been touched. a little frightened doe of a girl. easy to trick into turning her back. I raise a rusty shovel high above her head. wake suddenly while swinging downward. she's resigned to her own fate. doesn't forget herself. the other full of dreams. this isn't harmful he assures her. in fact it's the only way. wasn't it a smile. her first impulse. dizziness then dread. a word of this. if spoken. after a life of twisted weeds. she hasn't defeated anything. outran anything. now swirling in her stomach. similarities. differences. none of what she'd desired.

It may begin as reassuring as a heartbeat. any face but this that stands before me now. this dot sprouts fingers. philosophies. drowns him out. the runt claims similarities. hopes to appeal to their sense of brotherhood. he trudges onward like a factory. licks clean every spoon. I don't treat her badly. I won't apologize. next time I'll leave for good. I was a squanderer. spent all of my time there. inhaling the fumes. my own dissent. if these are her fears. something that could be manipulated. music to me. if she could only keep her mouth shut. some time to let the fruit ripen. words begin to penetrate the walls of his cocoon. I gave her a false name. whatever popped into my head. somehow it fit me. meltingly blessed. I need encouragement from him if I'm to continue with any confidence. even if I suspect his judgment being clouded. or worse yet. his dishonesty to spare me. the weekend passes. it remains empty. I grudgingly draw snail's blood. he gestures for her to speak louder. the little I know of her history has been mixed into a thick paste. a place I've been where the chaotic birds form single-file lines. I speak as little as possible in hopes of hastening my farewell. she's in love with this idea. a view of the rooftops that makes them look moveable. an age inducing joy. both of us saw him. the fear of the defenseless. a desperate faith in mercy. a breathless talonless buzzard bowing his apologetic head. weep. where are we going. is it cold there in the winter. what's down these stairs. brings out the same in me. the blinding glow in which things begin. I view it all with a detached eye. I'm numbed to the cries. she doesn't think he should be forgiven. I search for shadows. flickers. anything that might cause me to overlook his crimes. I find only selfishness. ignorance. his own comfort. it was never my intention. merely motion. oblivious of consequence. like birds sing. had meant to speak to me. pushed and pulled until all was forgotten.

I feel certain everything'll be fine for us. I won't tell her. she'd think I was only looking for excuses. she finds reasons to worry. things to surrender to. she doesn't understand that I'm blessed. that we'll be spared regardless. I won't complain. I'll never wish anyone harm. what is it about them. where it collects. how it holds on as if it were alive. he can be seen through. it can be assumed he wouldn't understand. her face disappears underneath an umbrella. she'll be this way forever. if I could see myself like this. someone who can't feel. has already exhausted every possibility. what I could've been if I were born here. I shade my eyes. I'm floating above my body. how does it look to them. it lasts beyond death. not a single drop's wasted. what'll we talk about while we're waiting. why she chose this color. what better way to show how little I care. I'll aspire to this. freedom. movement without results. invisible hands will catch us and lay us gently on the ground. it hurts. it makes the distance seem so great. what a terrible joke to play on them. putting this in their possession. I envision it. I mustn't overdo it. talks of himself being cursed. of feeling that it was his duty. why would she be here. what would've drawn her to him. she can't be found. this heart stops. we become too aware of each other. I'm back there. rubbing my eyes. I'm told to walk up and down the rows. to inspect every inch. take my time. they hold their breaths. they've been trained since birth. I was as bad as any other. I haven't killed it. I just keep it hidden away. I've never had a choice. if it were only us left. if fire swallowed everything else. if we had to begin again from scratch. could I be certain that she'd choose me. I'd be of no help. I'd weave in and out of the ribs of the skeletal remains. what if I've missed something. what if these stairs continue upwards forever. what if she's just how I remember her. it's the first time. she knew I'd come. she hasn't aged a day.

141

She's only slightly to blame. a thought that hadn't occurred. they've done it again. will claim it's an emergency. I wish I had lied. I still remember the last time. soaked to the bone. hoping he'd guide me through it. place me in the warmth. this potential. this time. this body. these distinguishing characteristics. I won't venture out beyond there. I won't approach her. these days are beautiful. the sun. the slight breeze. kept all day in a shoebox. playfully kicks when teased. returns for what he left behind. a deep vast silence can be broken by this. a bird's chirp. a tap on the window. I wonder if she has any more bad news. there's something on her mind. he asks dozens of questions in fear of being ignored. I'm much like this mist to him. a temporary comfort. a place to sit until hunger draws him away. is she enjoying this. some stay for hours. scarcely speaking. she stands behind him looking over his shoulder as he paints the clouds and treetops. the same way that he apologizes. requiring care. she passes gently into the following morning. comes up with an excuse to intrude. marks an X over something. locks the door. nervously. softly. I've remembered her name. imagine her lips to my ear. a glimpse of her smooth stomach. safe under layers of mousetraps. I'm once again in this position. have I dedicated enough time. been sincere. can I sigh with relief. express gratitude. still could be nothing at all. I see only his back. imagine the expression on his face. a dreamy-eyed sense of achievement. finally here. a slight chill. she thinks he needs a haircut. some new clothes. doubts whether all of their hearts are beating. the ones that look lost. that look sad. I'm usually able to control myself. take only furtive glances. only a dull impulse to flee. a cool afternoon. he'd wasted the morning. I've misplaced my faith. my trust. what was supposed to have steadied me. it makes me happy to fail so miserably. it makes me feel alive.

I hope she's sad today. I hope she's being watched. that he sees she's ordinary. I protect her from this distance. I sweep up the tiny shards of glass so she won't cut her feet. a devotion that's boring. especially to her. I wish there were a real threat. I wish the skin were softer. he wants to know the source of her resiliency. isolate it. keep it in a jar. watch it turn different colors. press his cheek against the glass. am I too sensitive. is this rejection. does it make me stronger. have I got things backward. should I be moving closer. this way it feels wonderful. nothing but time. he doesn't know any better. won't catch me off guard. things are right just as they are. I may outlive him. we'll finally be even. she's testing me. always gets home safely. from where I ponder blamelessly I sentence her to this. nothing comes naturally. everything takes concentration. what'll I say if she asks what I was doing there. when I've returned a different man. a trace left. the strange shadow I cast. finally reaching her. what we'd hoped for. only me. an accusing warmth. worth ten of her. the unlikeliness that she'd chase him. it's still on my tongue. experience. nothing left to chance. I wrongly consider this my reward. wherever she keeps it. humming softly. disagree as to its meaning. I'm the same person I was. I do the same things. how can this be of any interest to anyone. she's unhappy then she gets better. I'm unhappy then I get better. some days it's terrible. it frightens us. I need my privacy. they judge me too harshly. I've never tried at anything. I'm buried under thousands of baby bird skulls. I can't find my wallet. I'm growing older. these are the teeth marks. these are the vocal cords. she does her best. I'm not free. it can't be simply extracted. is accepting this a compromise. I do as much as I can. I pass the hours. I begin and finish things. there's no depth to it. there's no reason to look closer. where I've been placed. what's been designated mine.

143

I'd call it jealousy. anything that beautiful. whatever isn't required. I've only inherited part of this. some of the attributes. the ability to fool others. a mistrust. his enthusiasm. she's growing more certain of her purpose. why does it make me squirm. I'll probably disappoint them. what doesn't quite exist. what she strains to see. an insincerity I'd never meant to feel or display. it began. bad timing. stupid questions. or something entirely different. what she'd never confront him about. this form of selfishness. his true intentions. the hallway's dead silent. as is the stairway. as is the street. the color I'd like these walls to be. maybe even the glass in the windows. something more lifelike. she reaches out to me but stops there. she'll stay but it'll feel as if she'd walked away. as if she'd fallen over the edge of something. sailing downward. a smile on her lips. the day will come. the baby-soft concrete beneath. there must be some sound. any sound. sleep's useless. unreliable. I maneuver myself into position while no one's looking. it'd be wasted on them. some are dozing. hiding behind newspapers. is there a small place for him in her heart. what do I care. he thinks with embarrassment. when I'm alone. when she's not around. the smallest problems become insurmountable. when should I expect her. the clothes have dried. it's past lunch. I've emptied all of the wastebaskets. I need some fresh air. all day trying to bend him in that dank little room. it throws its weight around. it takes him from me. returns him slightly different. something like our life together settles into place. if I ever did give an answer. how it'd rouse him from this stupor. I cross a bridge. I sail past darkened doorways. I stop to admire her face. cheekbones. eyes. I knew how to possess this. it slides down my throat. all this was built for me. to leave its indentation on my skin. I'm a blood cell pumping through its veins. its vitality.

I wanted both pairs of hands to caress me at once. we've become so selfish now that movement's possible. a timidity she attributes to restraint. she becomes someone else. a gradual change. I resent these accusations. I stood aside and let her have exactly what she said she wanted. how she sees it. used him to scare me. only a little is required. I lay down on my stomach and press my face to the floor. I welcome him to place his foot on by back. to pose as if he's won a decisive victory. I'll pretend I'm out cold. I think of what I'd meant to them. how I felt I'd deserved to be included. what I understand now that she's a stranger. no longer spared her viciousness. I could be next. I can explain everything. I stop dead in my tracks. the murky waters in which I'd drowned her now up around my knees. I fall apart. I'm trying to justify a crime I hope I someday have the nerve to commit. what has she told him. why is it unforgivable. the harmless way dead leaves fall. the threatening way he looks at me. I know everything. I had to listen to it over and over again. I had to wait until she was emptied. I try to be honest. it's still buried. I'd have given myself entirely. I'm pushing them all toward this. it pains him to watch her leave. with my imagination. with my tongue. what eventually happens to all wounds. her hand in mine. she pretends she never thought of it. I deal with him this way. it hibernates. it eats its storage of food. I inspire nothing. I hide in here when it becomes too demanding. too sorrowful or joyous. too confusing or too clear. I nail boards over the windows. I can carry on for months. even she doesn't suspect a thing. envy is eating my compassion. I won't allow the truth in though it rattles the door in its hinges. I want this kind of poverty. this particular need. he'll never be held accountable. he can say and do whatever he pleases. he can cross back and forth over this imaginary line. he'll be loved for no other reason other than that he was born.

145

Another building's being erected just outside my window. it'll completely block out my view of the sky. I can hear the drilling now. earlier I watched the workers eating and laughing. what'll it be. will I ever have a reason to enter. when she's tired I can see how weak her faith is. how much effort it takes to pretend. it's not like her to keep me waiting. they'll confuse me for one of the gutter rats. alone among the broken eggshells. perhaps the last time I'd ever see him. waves goodbye from a second story window. I'd leave him to die there. her patient little heart. forever hopeful. I'm trying to prove my level of devotion. nearly broke my neck on the fire escape. the sooner I finish the sooner I can leave. the sooner they'll be swallowed whole. dissolved by stomach juices. I'm moving too slowly. a feeling that sometimes settles on me. it comes from without. do I lack dedication. do I look foolish to them. moping around the puddles. letting days pass fruitlessly. stretched out. talking. was frightened when she saw what was floating there. I want to take everything from him. he needs to be stimulated. she watches him brush the crumbs from her plate into his palm. a short embrace the next morning. an attempt to say he's sorry for what's still to come. these acts of kindness leave me feeling invaded. behind a closed door I'm much closer to sincerity. less insulted. dreams of faraway places where they're too exhausted to fight back. there are no similarities between us. I see some splash against his face. I believe it's what he wants. that the screams of frustration are for my benefit. they've declared a winner. he's humiliated. a slave to their every whim. this is my new life. I spread my things all over the floor. I extend my arms and don't knock anything over. I care if I keep them awake. should I feel guilty for choosing this path. who's stirring at this late hour. she was here today. she helped me unpack. makes me happy. I assume it's good.

146

I'm lying on the floor like a dog. the train goes by. if I died she'd hold my drawings to her chest. should impatience merit punishment. her fondest memories. her vertebrae. the tiny gears that make the clock tick. an ugly lonesome ritual. he'll pretend to have forgotten this. any excuse to turn toward me. look at my face. feel vaguely like he's lost something. walk sadly away. she's locked out. the key could be anywhere. the places she passes through. so unlike him. simply drained. pricks up his ears. he doesn't know I'm watching. realizes it's cold. zips his jacket all the way up. crosses the street. is fabricating a story. has to get up early. would they hear if I went splat. seems an easy thing to do. takes him a whole year. beautiful little diamond shapes. the smallest sounds echo in here. have tastes. my insides. smaller than my fist. pink as my gums. invisible. may be turning black. do I admire her honesty. do I think too little of him. breathes life into my illusions. gives me a reason to leave the house. I can't speak or understand the language. it's liberating. the tiny steps I take are met with great joy. it's always assumed I mean well. I'm never distracted by others' conversations while reading on the train. he gives half answers. he knows his loneliness interests me. and after he's returned from there. exactly what time. he's worse off than I was. I plod down the hall. I settle into it like a bath. we've reached an agreement. held gently to her lips. the things it's best she doesn't hear. watching them multiply. I sigh selfish and cruelly. dig my fingers into the carpet. her scent in my nostrils. who she brought with her. even stranger. thin as a straightened coat hanger. why did I leave. I could've waited for her. it wouldn't have been long. I'd fall back asleep. I'd stir as she re-entered. we're alone now. she's transformed. it doesn't mean anything. I never completely enjoy myself. begin scattering. returning to dust.

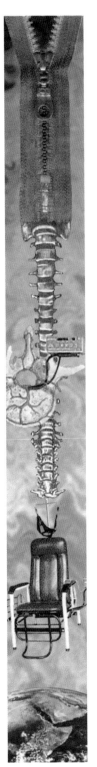

147

I can see the backs of their heads. I want to sneak up behind him. whisper in his ear. it never happened. it's never going to happen. it's the first time I've gone outside in days. I want it over with as soon as possible. I want to return home. my first desires. to be remembered. to have some authority. I only acknowledge failure. surround myself with other failures. don't trust anyone who's had success. they must've sold their souls. committed heinous crimes. I hear a familiar laugh. know he's approaching. how they never let anyone change. keep them in picture frames. beside herself with this. voiced openly. aimlessly through former bedrooms. was her faith so inordinate. I know he's here. has risen above the other sardines. my heart was bigger then. I don't even like them anymore. what would've become of me if I'd stayed. would it've been so terrible. they don't dread the future like I do. they sleep like logs. I cave inwards. won't leave them. they're bickering. a soft knock at the door. I couldn't help but notice. I have nothing else to occupy my mind. she begins each morning by marking another X through a day on the calendar. an office piled high with symbols. she succumbs to this anxiety. crawls into her fortress. must move quickly. burn the evidence. he visits every day. it's obvious to me. jumps at the slightest sound. coughs like a dying man. hardly misses the things of his she just to spite him threw away. I was wearing a uniform. a lovely day to be in the park. they're no match for me. fools who spill from piano benches. every moment precious. I'm too old for her. I've brought myself to look at him. I want these days to end. she got home safely. so cold that night. has been for years her shackles. moves accordingly. dies after its first little frog hop. imagines the shape of its own emptiness. how it burns through intestines. blankets. pillows. sleepless hours. remembrances. I used to have so many friends.

I've seen rats in here. they crawl in through this hole. they bravely brush against my feet as I sit at my desk. they take themselves seriously. challenge each other. I wouldn't know him if he bit me. she offers suggestions. douses me with water. I've exhausted her patience. seen from this angle. grizzly. wide-awake on the dissection table. hands search for inspiration. simple disgust in their eyes. my mind allowed to wander. it finally dribbles downward. they grab what they came for. leave the room like rapists. my uneventful life continues. to confess this to anyone. what exactly. the choice to remain as this. to have no illusions about people. what we know better than to desire but still spin with the uncertainty. the ointment of our fears rubbed into our skin. where had been protective scales. she was dead wrong. he's drawn at times to the holes in their fences. pasts and futures flung recklessly aside. true love. digested. forgiven. he says he doesn't like to think about it. hides inside a laughter through which the squeaking wheels can be heard. I don't have the strength to ignore them. asked questions. so must speak. she ate a little food this morning. has given them cause for hope. he licks the tears from my cheeks before they reach my chin. she doesn't see the dangers. a few months' time. more of the same. I don't trust him. she waves this aside. he's grown soft over there. has seen much worse. was fortunate. a lulling sound. the way she enters rooms. the only time I've ever heard him allude to how things had become the way they were. how long ago the ice began to form. differed from what he'd hoped. began to spread. I know what displeased him. men like that. when someone isn't awed. don't suppress it. a grace. how crippling guilt can be. unless he was lying. why would he. much smaller in real life. that which unites them. attracts me to each. he's grown too weak to stand. what lead her to me. and on and on. these rituals. this realization.

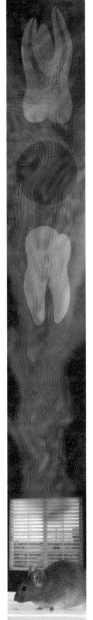

149

I prefer one to the other. a less humiliating defeat. and if he hadn't taken me aside. expressed his concerns. inquired as to her whereabouts. she's left. he understands me. she's beautiful in what she's able to keep concealed. I'm better than him. if not I'd still be in her arms. as a favor to him I fill in the blanks. I squeeze between his body and the mirror. part of me wants to ring his neck until the polka dots are shaken loose and float upwards. another part of me plunges into the shame. the gray and seaweed. the softness between my toes. I've snuck my hatchet in. it'll go thunk in his side as if he were a log. a relief to hear he's lost this. has ruined their evening. crumbles under such demands. I feel stronger. he detects this. lunges for my throat. a manner of speaking. I pretend to have a vague recollection of it. used to happen weekly. as though I were giving them a gift. crushed one beneath my heel. nearing oblivion. swirling wings and arms. can one be expected to care. during that time moved with great caution. on tiptoes. well kept. enhancing each morning. my weakened condition. I struggled to share this with her. a fraction. in hopes of blossoming. killed in its infancy as it should've been. is bound to be. our introduction. unspeaking. slouched against a wall that separates nothing from nothing. I'm forgetting something. rack my brain. what I'm afraid of. his suggestions. flip-flopping between playfulness. a moment of her time. and growing dread. is she safe. is she able to breathe. these questions. if I'm allowed to intervene. but beyond me. repetition. the three of us like cuckoo clocks. it's been a bad day. because she complained. the reason why some people were put here. I can't go on. the thanks I get. the others standing idly by. a nerve she hit. a threat. after all young and defenseless. what it's meant to them. the queasiness. my will dripping out. together they're a nightmare. I'm in for much worse. I wake and have to return there again.

My life has changed. I hurry home at the end of each day. work's nearly unbearable. I correct myself. it's only the past. is lifted off me as I come through the door and I know she's there at the end of the hallway. humming to herself. chopping vegetables. the warm glow from all around her. no one has feelings in the real world. they just do their jobs. I can kick them and they won't bruise. not even a reaction. I can push them in front of oncoming trains. they'd fall just as carefree as limbs cut from trees. there are some pulses. some thoughts. they're gathered around the newsstand. I jostle one with my elbow as I push through. when he was young. her name swallowed up by this thickness. I watched it spread. is the nature of these things. a sweet little wide-eyed voice. what she uses as a tool. I have no choice. do what's expected. a weight laid on top of me. this opportunity. a way to make her happy. even the ones that despised me. circled around. wondered how we met. this landscape. strange to think. the objects lining these shelves. here they are. so unified. a first. it occurred to me. never once if dozens of lifetimes passed would I do such a thing. and where was she. what did she make of this. and them. must find at once. physically. possibilities that exist. pictured it. was full of dread and shame. but I need to be thinking something. what I'd allowed myself. it's limitless. one's soul. a still warm corpse ravaged by beasts. all of this applauded. if what she's done in the past. regardless of how little sense it makes to me now. or if I can even remember clearly the events and thoughts that led her there. still has some effect on me. won't allow itself undone. her identity. these acts. so completely. nod knowingly. intertwined. a break must be violent. spoken harshly. and if I'd have found her. how could she let this happen. many more times. my heart sank as such. often miscalculating. a smooth place that could've been her cheek.

Once the leaves in the trees. and the grass. all the same color. green. blown softly. he expects me to disagree with my usual lack of eloquence. seems disappointed I'm remaining silent. behaving like a shadow. seeing him smile. behind him insects climb the walls. were they my imagination. tranquility. gentleness. the petals of this flower scattered across the nightfall. I too have these feelings. if they stick to the bottom of my shoes I'll bring them with me down the alley. leave them in piles in the gutters. so unfitting an end. so noble an effort. he's been rubbed the wrong way. must remember not to make such rude requests. unaccustomed as I am to acts of charity. he'd never make it to work the next day. didn't ask about what'd happened in his absence. only stared at the fish in the fish tank. accuses me of not appreciating the subtleties. quite possibly. nothing to be learned here once the initial charm's worn off. he was relaxing. the other was restless. not only tonight but overall. driven by this boredom. these needs. she led me down the street to a locked door. wants us to bang our fists against it. scream of injustice. I taste it. I knew what was coming. what'll spring forward in me. what'll come out when I open my mouth. how I'm different from them. that this isn't really what I want. how all day every day I fantasize about escaping. what I've banished from my memory. and all desire to allow it again. unthinkable. and yet what had occurred. should we be ashamed of ourselves. do we have any control. are some free of such concerns or do they drag them into the daylight to have a better look. the sky's blue but the clouds look thin and sinister. just like bones. it's painless. it's a mistake to abandon this for confusion and noise. something'll present itself. I'm certain. he's on his way to her. enjoying the train ride. watching people from above. just like a bird. and repeats this. not so rarely tempted. a twisted pride in it. I suppose.

The night condenses things. events unfold in flashes that in the daytime would take hours. I'm in awe. and even further wonders. I brag like an idiot. what people do when they're lonely. before too much time's been wasted. in this crawl space. wait patiently. like clothing. she kissed my elbow and left. I can conjure her up. she's singing to herself. she'd never let this happen. times like this. worse can be forgiven. oceans of us. go about a normal life. I want an answer. this more slowly. I relaxed my jaw. let my fists unfold. underwater plants. a near caress that I could swim through. before these eyes his childhood swelled and overcame his greed. if something could be done to make the days pass more quickly. until she were here. lying with my belly exposed. staring off. blue and red dots. the end of another day. if this bulb flickered then went black. could it lead me there. an all-consuming hunger. a bowl of plastic fruit. closer to her. he's been proven innocent. took it all in stride. I'm happy to be wrong. one day driven forward. beyond and then above. who do I thank. sang all the way home. more than a drop. a set of footprints. rocking in my cradle. what's happened to my sister. I'd already known. still talking to the empty space long after he was gone. she overflows. joy. the corners of her eyes. youthful glow. where he's frozen. open arms and falling snowflakes. a child born to a child. the heart and soul of it. made windows rattle. I claimed it as my own. slipped it over my face. given a glimpse of this side of me he turned and walked away. the filthy thing now in my hand. she cheated. I still feel as if she owns a part of me. where rusting cheer and belief is kept. where something has come to an end. taken apart piece by piece. may as well pity her. pause a moment. enter a room. there's no evidence but it's true. I stumble down the stairs and into the early morning air. my cheeks and ears are cool. my fingers move clumsily over buttons. I nearly get hit by a car.

153

I always recover. my stomach settles down. my eyelids droop. it's natural. I take possession of her. I think about how unlikely it is. how unlikely anything is. what insistently transpires regardless of what I do. if I were born rich I'd find some other way to make life painful. if I ever achieved anything I'd still find something wrong with it. there's a logic to my stillness. I see how they move and wonder if I haven't lived. if I haven't been raised to quietly look on. what's the truth. sometimes I feel they hate me. others that they mustn't have any doubt I hold this all together. I repeat the words in my head until they become a presence. something with eyes. until I fall asleep. what'll I do after this. it has even less of a chance. how'll I teach them not to fail. what can I possibly say. I go there and disappear. rest my head. let the wind take me. I only care about her. and eating. I'll let all of this die. my stomach grumbles all the way home. I have no discipline. no pride. I pinned it to the wall and threw darts at it. what good am I. I want to be carried the rest of the way. I see bony things pass underneath streetlights. peering in shop windows. he wouldn't understand. it was easier then. there was no cause for hesitation. it's finally my turn. her days must be exhausting. laughter. her shoulders. her neck. pretending to honor this. dozens of them. more each day. this one specifically. its cause. ever present. a stone's throw. loyalty has led me here. made my heart explode. she could never be that straightforward. learned to love whatever was left. no money or food and still we must sacrifice. this jacket does nothing against the cold. I'm trespassing. disturbing the peace. soon they'll drop like flies. afternoons of sadness. she'd be unfairly placed with me. evaporate. the only thing that continues to grow. believed in his heart that this much could be salvaged. that she'd return to him if released from its grip.

There's no furniture in this room yet. there're no bad memories. everything's been burned. he sits outside. that one's her window. it'll be enough. I'll survive the winter through thievery. fear keeps things in their place. crosses a busy street then becomes one of them. accepts his share of the blame. I could've slid. busted my head open. snapped my spine in two. sometimes I wonder if I didn't. I hope she cries. has to will herself to get out of bed. I keep my fingers crossed. time will bring new lows. shoveled in my mouth with a dirty spoon. innocent enough. what all others have coming. when my back heals. nonsense. nose to the grindstone. come home with nothing. I'm a dog on two leashes. he fears I've grown soft. I'm dismissed with a wave. in some way detect them. scratch too fiercely. bleed. if we just met yesterday. if I still had questions to ask. her unselfishness can be annoying. I'm attempting to revert to being a child. a way of thinking. a way of solving problems. they swarm him. stomp feet. laugh. I land a blow to the back of his head. leave him in a pile. I'm proud. I convince her she's also capable of this. then it runs on its own. a form of punishment. builds an elaborate backdrop. phony holes in the carpet. phony garbage cluttering the stairs. untied phony shoelaces. convincingly real heads and torsos made from eggshells and orange rinds. what flutters downward to me. nothing gives inspiration. I want to kick it. I wake and see my breath. I demand this of myself. she remembers him as this. unable to sustain anything for very long. stuttering. feigning ignorance. a mouth opened to receive. a bottomless pit. the door opens a crack. we all feel the chill. I'll drop soon. some sort of mental preparation. it'll get worse. it'd sicken me to see myself there. I see her late in the day and am reminded of a dream I had the night before. I'm always pressured. something I want to do but I shouldn't. she sits at my shoulder reading my mind.

155

I slide in beside her under the covers. my feet are freezing. I'm careful not to touch her. a disease I've brought into our room. I'm certain we won't fail. a deformity that comes with love. it'll be cold in the morning and we'll both have to work. she leaves a little before me. she's left her umbrella behind. it's my right to know how often such things happen. does he ever find anything in them other than desperation. all in the streets with the same needs. how's there ever any peace. two'll start by sneaking glances. don't breathe a word of it yet. I could do worse. buttoning today's shirt. the same tie. I'm a stupid animal. my reflection in a window. I need perspective. if he wasn't there and I could've ran. somehow behind myself. watching myself grow smaller. I made a mistake. a different shape. and from this distance. an open wound. chances best left squandered. I did better than some. lied to his face but never quit. earned some respect. my course is set. still dream of being called upon. yet lazy. stubborn. these days. I'm speaking to her. it gushes out of me like I've been cut open. I don't care what effect it has. I don't care if it doesn't make sense. it's too personal so I stop. there are other things. now I fill in their hearts. I put words in their mouths. I press my ear to the wall of the cocoon and try to hear whatever I can. a train passes mine in the opposite direction. the windows rattle violently. the noise is incredible. seems to last impossibly long. I don't have to work tomorrow. I can enjoy myself tonight. it's worse than simple hunger. it's a feeling of continuing on in the wrong direction. it can't be filled. it's twice the size of me. everything passes too quickly. she's gone by the time I've focused my attention. I feel like someone else. like a stranger. a person lying next to a person. I listen. I get up and walk down the hall. what'll I do. I don't mean from here onwards. right now. tonight. what'll I do if I don't want to lose my mind.

156

Once and for all I've erased them. then on the way home from work. more of the same. what became of me. the ones who've survived. the joy she brought to some. these immediate concerns. how I can't trust myself. she's blushing. what he usually pounces on. these charms. this happiness. everything that's fleeting. arrives with an empty heart. wonder gone. anger gone. this point in the evening. she's too easily awed. never one to interrupt. sped from its initial crawl. mid-life. he's leading us. silence. too many corners. becoming less likely. less capable. she and I are something taken by the wind and blow down distant streets. it no longer interests me. approaches from either side. inhale. exhale. both of us hate him. she pays close attention. my mind wanders. my head pops off. my skull bounces down a flight of stairs. I can achieve what I set out to do. nonsense. hours pass. he's impatiently tapping his foot. I'm not speaking to him. shoo him away. break a broomstick over his back. the other weaklings peel the blankets from their shoulders. mangy dogs. rot to death. the first to have gracefully dissolved. spends time with her sister. arranges them on the floor of her room. sat and looked. became bored. once more. then stood back. fills with delight. as close as we'd ever come to communication. for my part I drifted backwards. found the urge to make comparisons. almost certain it was her idea. the awkwardness it inspired. the questions in the air. we both recoil. give a meaningless and sudden laugh. takes himself away defeated. am I the only one who sees that none of this matters. nothing to give. grown up and dreamless. grabbed one from the tool shed. off to war. I've suppressed it in myself for too long. he's let it grow in him. obvious as a nose. pure and simple. a whimper I couldn't ignore. I don't want to have to choose between one and the next. memorize these lines. await my cues. I'm insulted. I shouldn't be. I should be able to see beyond this.

157

My head was on backwards. it superseded all other considerations. to what consequence. are there similarities. bruises. she wants to be alone. I can meet her in the morning and walk her to the train station. the pain isn't mine. disappears completely from my mind. only returns when I see her face. even then seems minor. almost pretend. am I convincing. always at these times. unworthy. but it wasn't a death. may prove to be a birth. she'll wait for me. I'll have no other choice. come to grips with the truth. may be far worse. more damaging. just from that point to this. from this window I can only see the tops of their heads. no one ever looks up. she begs but he doesn't stop. he enjoys it. doesn't swerve. I've created this. I've laid its foundations. nurtured it. led by example. put her in harm's way. everything at once being dragged through the mud. and I'd return. wide-eyed. eager. cooler heads prevailed. she walks on the surface. I'm submerged. a different man now. I feel it in my soul. the price I pay to exist. to commit other crimes. other types of seaweed. I'm never understood. silhouettes keep watch. my greatest fear. everything at once. and to parade it around before my eyes. to revel in it. she's absorbed. in security. in the realization that they have their own minds. all there is to know. what to avoid. not a single one would end up here. my current predicament. sighs of relief. messy. noisy bursts. why suddenly to me. a place she hardly ever went. and jealous of her faith in this. a fun house mirror. a part of me she'd no longer recognize. another part of me she'd wish had changed. what fun to disappoint her. I prefer pity to friendship. I don't share his allegiance. the thought of seeing them regularly. any amount of exoneration would never be enough. I'll withdraw even further. return on one condition. that it's all been taken from him. may be cowardice. or knowing my weaknesses. or the most useless kind of wisdom.

158

The furthest corners where it's crumbling. just this afternoon I thought of us running across the asphalt. avoiding broken glass. jumping over puddles. I remember when he admitted to stealing. I'd have never suspected him. the way she made him suffer. the way he's frozen. blubbering and red faced. his fair skin inflamed. her arms and fingers were so thin and her eyes so wide that at first it was impossible to think of her as anything other than an insect. I was afraid when they approached. too weary for talk. for giving off light and sound. but they returned stares with smiles. crossed to our table and sat down. she in a circular motion. him rather reluctantly. followed by another. bundled tight against the cold. lips that would remain sealed. I kick myself today. he's unwinding. he's seen the world. I know just where to find his heart. before the cave in. she only smiles. a brain in there somewhere. wrapped in soft fur. we'd been alone. a bit jumpy. it never made much sense. begins dancing. noticed us laughing. what we've stumbled upon. hands me a pretty blue bottle. wander further. flowers running up the neck. the way I'm sure that time is passing. taken away then soon replaced. stop worrying. a friendly face. a man who could move mountains. falling over themselves. clutching my wrist. spreads his arms and roars. soak it in. my lucky day. hang on his every word. it's cold and dark out there. I'd have never left. they waited for us near the door. I'd hoped we'd be friends. why has it stalled. the usual mid-morning noises. louder as they pass. and then the spaces left behind. there's a misunderstanding. we're forced to move. a moment they've violated. adhered to policy. I'd like to see her again. returning home. anything he wants. hours entirely his. no one's angry. I can handle the boredom. envision him the next morning. walking out into the sunshine. the door swings slowly shut. she leans against my shoulder.

159

He ignores me. remembers the past. fills with joy. I look at her confused silent face. the surrounding luxury. I run down the street to return to his side. my tongue's grown accustomed to this taste. it clings. we part in the cold just before dawn. I could've followed them. warmed myself by the source of their certainty. she'd pressed her spine against mine. quelled my fears. my petty concerns. I was eager to praise them. gushed each time. she watched me closely. I couldn't be sincere. I want to corrupt her. to expose the futility of her pursuits. reconstruct her soul. make her conform to these ideals. it's taken all this time for me to finally learn what I'm incapable of. he's still not answering. I'll stir this in her. she'll build us a little fortress. any of them'll do. an honest mistake. she'd no right to slap him. the long stretch of silence. apology. the sickly breath. all those who don't believe I can succeed. all those standing in my path. the mess on the train platform. running late today. knowing the reason. I can't picture her face. just the colors she was wearing. her hands. her voice. I wonder if I should say anything. the less talk the better. thinking's enough. if fear or timidity leaves things unaltered. one's still guilty. has still strayed from virtue. but if so what's to stop us. I wouldn't have otherwise. partially just to prove her wrong. to throw it back in her face for having guided me so recklessly. there's a distinction. our thoughts and our deeds. the prisons would be bursting. how perhaps she envisions it. packed in tightly. another would agree to meet me. let me kiss her. compared to moments he looks off somewhere blankly. mouthing words. something that's been stuck in my head. I could feel how thin her neck was. the softness of her hands. that's why he's lifeless. tries not to fantasize. is it possible I've exhausted this idea. is it best to stop now. but what happens after that. another morning would come. I'd awake and have no purpose.

What if one of these thoughts forced its way through her mind. spun a web there. if she acted on the urge to hide it underneath her coat and walk quickly toward the door. she's angry. little by little it's all disappearing. the spaces in between have grown. have consumed what was touchable. I scratch her face off. now an empty white oval. I'm somewhere in the middle. smiling. she was right all along. I've stopped being offended. at these times it's almost worth something. the two of us on display. I should be suspicious. she's attempting to pry him loose. how long can I keep this up. what hope is there for me. I've allowed us to drift here. to be covered over. I've tied the strands together. I'll wait until she breaks. I saw him last night. he's slipping. a symptom of what's deeper. what's meant by this. are these possibilities. I'm shaking like a man forced to steal. they just keep moving. I could be going anywhere. in the train station. near the center. near the statue of the owl. I haven't considered what comes next. it's cold. I can see my breath. I take the slip of paper from my wallet. look at her handwriting. weren't there lines around her eyes. I've made a decision. she'll be late and I'll feel foolish. then I finally see her. who'll he be tonight. alone. unmonitored. with money in his pocket. why's she crying. anyone else would've tried to console her. warm her. even if they knew that it wasn't this bad. that she was overreacting. seemed my only response. he's pulling me downward. he needs a companion without hope or pride or strength. I'm teaching her a lesson. building her character. there were times he praised me. applauded my efforts. defended me when I was attacked. but then his reproaches. more severe as time passed. our last encounter. he's become more complex. if it were her there at that moment. and she'd listen. I've been dreaming. nothing accomplished. never knowing what became of this devotion. I'm not curious. one of millions.

I should be home in bed. the rain's soaked into my shoes. I'm watching them form lines. make decisions. and then my stomach's full. I enter through the front door. he's alright. let him pass. trailing rain up the stairs. let him gather what he can. she's disrupted my morning. such demands are never made of me. I know a shortcut. the bricks wobble underneath my feet. the sun nearly blinds me. swallows her whole. I've seen her up close. he's tired of her. what it's really like. how everyone's misled. it wouldn't be right for her to be young. it puts me at ease. the wind grabs hold of everything. it's easy for me to place her there. if one finds this enticing. makes an entrance. goes to her usual corner. devours them. stacks of them. he can never forget her. she leaves. the little bell rings. in floats the smells from the street. I'm crying because I lost my job. things have not gone well since I've come back. they're at each other's throats because of me. he just sits there. he'd starve to death if not for us. the mirror's angled so that I can see whoever's approaching. an unfamiliar face is framed then wanders off. if I'd have stayed like she'd suggested. if we were alone when my eyes popped open. if I could've forgiven things. she's lost in this clutter. she's agreed to it. she's smiling. almost weightless. murmuring in her sleep. I'm collecting her movements. another's watching. she isn't jealous. hasn't taken off her coat yet. we've stopped eating. we've sworn. until our bones are clanking together. we've become like sisters. brush each other's hair. she doesn't know anything about the outside world. she just listens. doesn't age. didn't come from anywhere. always seems to know what I'm thinking. where I want her to be. when I'm hoping she'll come closer. I'm peeling away what I don't need. what's left are outlines. a few things they've said that have survived. we were separated. only warm thoughts. these are the broken pieces. what puts words in my mouth.

Great importance has been placed on this. the necessary half-truths. I'm recovering from this apathy. I've gathered evidence. if I never grew hungry or didn't need to sleep. he's losing himself in this quest. to be carefree. to justify his desires. but just like with everything else he's not sure if it's what he wants. she's resigned to this. waits for the day when he finally emerges. I insist it remains in a box near my bed. I don't want her to understand. I'm cradling this dissonance. allowing it to eat from my hand. she's my only link to humanity. however much she's alive within them. she doesn't accept this in others because it's never existed in her. they're all the same. able to rationalize things. lie to each other. then once outside. the few unknowing souls who've been freed. how could I have known him my entire life and never even seen a flicker. I don't suspect he's keeping secrets. I don't think he's ever even tempted. these are his flaws. it's made us stronger. I wasn't around most of the time. felt none of the tension. was lazing about a safe distance away. she's there to listen. the sensation of sinking. I can't answer her. the reasons we aren't speaking. it's better than fighting. him raising his voice. it's his fault. everything. from the beginning of each day until the end. I've never been much help. I've corrupted them. it's better now that I'm not needed there. he was jealous of something I've always taken for granted. something I only see the value of now. my greatest fear is suffering a blow to this. its strength and consistency. others find ways to survive. stick together. I'm the opposite. he never says anything comforting. gives only if I beg. it'll get worse. even less. increasingly dull. he's simplified this. a role he plays. the least amount required. it's a side effect. my past. the things I've gathered that he smashes one by one. they feel it too. where others attach romance. endure strife. live only to conceal it.

163

If I could be certain of this. that these fears rise in everyone. how much more tolerable life would be. I curse myself. wait for the light to change. the happy memories from this time. showering them with presents. sitting back with my feet up. but her always being there. I felt like a goldfish. in his laughter the sound of someone starving hoping to be offered food. these formalities. I say something. I worry. the extent to which it's true. I've sabotaged my future. an attempt to wipe things clean. she's given as much consideration as the raindrops that beat somewhere high above my bed. he doesn't understand what makes them afraid. why they deny themselves. why they belittle him. what makes them bend. accept this praise and emptiness for their subservience when even the worst possible outcome of being individual and honest is comparatively mild. shall we be enemies. will he feed me. the most recent coat of paint's begun to peel. what I've always pictured for us. peace. satisfaction. rest. there's only one chair. one glass. one pair of shoes. a wind that could've blown gently has now torn everything down. I've failed. I'll try again. someone'll be with me then. I won't regret my life. I'll move forward. I haven't told them anything. she was sworn to secrecy but I'm sure she's filled them in. never mind. in ways yet to recover. this is her solution. I'll compromise what little dignity I've been left. they'll be let down. pick the flesh from me. this should be abandoned. any further thoughts of this. only pain and surrender. how'll I occupy my evenings. will the silence have a calming effect or will I race to where things blur. should I be thinking this. our life would be more hers than mine. I see my name near the top of a letter she's writing. there's a devil or something on my shoulder. still more things to weed through. think back to who I was. when she's digging in the back of the closet for something. when I'm asked where she is.

164

I could've done or said anything. I can sense her anger. I see through everything now. I've denied myself this simple pleasure. everything's a threat. what does it make me. I want to see and listen again with innocence. I want to find where I turned. I don't mean it. then what would I use to beat them off. I'm at my worst. peel everything away and am still left with lies. I don't trust myself. I don't trust her. find a place. stay until I die. I've assumed this about him. that he's trying to break my concentration. she embodies this rejection. she proves that I haven't grown. I find ways to go back. watch things burn and curl. I'm there again. it doesn't matter what she believes. I open and shut her eyes. blow air into her lungs. take and scatter me here. let me stick to her. I carry it. it helps me make decisions. I'm a terrible employee. my heart isn't in it. the day ends and I leave. I always lose. walk away as fast as I can. he hopes I'll be inspired. that I'll respond well to the challenge. I can't stop doubting my judgment. every movement I make. I'm nervous the entire day. I don't want anything from them. I come home and eat. I have to go back the next day. I set foot in there and am consumed by this. the feeling of having nothing to give. I've been trying to care for years. for myself. they can think whatever they want. she wants me to say more. I'm an empty vessel. it's worse than she imagines. I'm so far from where I want to be. I have to change everything. I have to tell them the truth. I'd like to see all of this burned. I want him brought down to my level. I want to see her stripped of her resources. he has something to hide. walks on eggshells. if my existence could be unobserved. if I weren't responsible for strengthening or weakening the whole. how can I impress them. ease their minds. I don't allow it in. grind my teeth. drift off. stop to rest under a tree. lie all the way back. watch ants carrying tiny bits of food.

165

I'll never prove them wrong. it'll go on and on until one of us decides it should end. she crumbles. unlike her. no one'll ever take our side. years'll pile up and where'll we go to escape. it's not only her. it's all of them. today'll be better. I'll let that part of me die. she gave up on me. why is it important. I'm being erased. defeat upon defeat. no one to share this with. there used to be dozens of us. she wanted to leave but I wanted to stay. I let her win. we drift through the souvenir stands. halfway down the street I beg to go back. I want to know more about them. I want to gaze until my curiosity's satisfied. she's enamored with some little trinket. keeps turning it over and over in her hands. hears my voice from far off behind her somewhere. a golden opportunity. we're letting it slip away. she's digging in her purse for coins. I want to be with someone else. it's as black and white as if it were written on paper. this fundamental difference. what I've fought against for too long. despite the beauty that sails past me. despite what I'm digesting. there's sorrow. my devotion dribbles down my spine. something's pulling me toward this solution. it's weakness to acknowledge this world. it's a crime. the shine I put on this. what'd be unforgivable in others. I want to be left alone. I owe them my time because I want food and warmth. because I have to take care of her. a picture a child drew. too much of one color. if these two dreams could collide. stuttering and stupid questions. they'd adore him. I spoke more of her yesterday than I had in the past four years. she's nothing like I remember. I crawled under here to hide from the adults. to rest my head on the soft carpet. I turn and stare up at the underside of the table. I'm seeing something forbidden. what they've conspired to keep secret. she wants me to explain. she's the only who's ever asked. I'm not above jealousy. it's driven deeper into me. she's as light on her feet as a mouse.

166

I see her off then am alone with the chirping insects. what was the reason for her change of heart. it'd seemed a possibility. other times something destined. I wish I could take back words. I live turned away from her. she left with all my hope. all my sympathy. I waited until disgust set in then made my way to bed. what's holding me back. drifted out even further. when I become selfish and the boundaries blur. I'll go there tomorrow. she'll forgive me. she'll have to. he's lost in thought. one by one sends them away. where was she when I was hungry. every detail's important. her hands. her jewelry. I notice if something's missing or if something new appears. life'll bow down to her. misfortunes'll whither and drop. it'd kill me to watch. it's a relief she's gone. this love. the only thing that daunts me. does it ease up. will it remain. wrap itself around my neck. they'll talk. for now. before their towers fall. before something new's revealed. I'll be given purpose then. as I've always done. jump from stone to stone. the thuds on empty skulls. my smile warmly returned. somehow we've remained intact. I'll take her to a place where the hammering can't be heard. this area of town. how I was temporarily charmed. soothed. questioned. he'll keep his wits about him. if I were allowed to lay down between them. this lightness. like another person. counts the days. falls into traps. shuns comfort. not all love is as fleeting as ours. theirs is something different. someone with whom it doesn't seem a chore. I must cease to view this as my last chance at fulfillment if I'm not to repeat his mistakes. anything about them. any kind of resolution. she prefers silence. drugged by this stillness. it seemed childish not to love her. to need something else. how it felt when she finally forgave. I could've chosen either one. who was responsible. what were their thoughts. pieces break off. I've convinced her she should accept less. places we've killed time. those who've passed through.

167

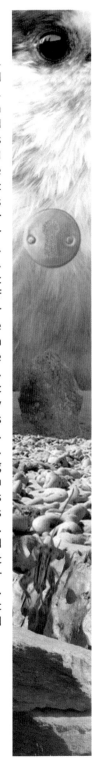

Then at last. in alarm. finds himself at her feet. from my window I watch them pass by underneath. an absurdity. a reminder. sings to herself. if she had him alone. what we're doomed to. I can walk there. gather her up in my arms. sleep all afternoon. not the only prying eyes. check the wrist for a pulse. beauty lives in fear of time. we're lost. we're afraid of ourselves. the ways we've grown. these decisions. but it all continues. it carries on for years. there's light. she'll leave at some point. any further. I'm incapable. she's just as careless. just as injury prone. throw away this life together. how he sat me down. asked me not to interrupt. said it'd make perfect sense. I know he's gone for good. he was gone before he left. another face in my head. a space cleared. this means nothing. my crowning achievement. she places the blame on me. I can smell her. taste her frustration. soon to be pouring from this gash. I won't be bitter. life'll start again. is it simple anger or a debilitating wound. an attempt to release me. how little he understands. as if I haven't had time to think. or what I've seen shouldn't affect this. the concern on their faces. how they've imagined this moment. what they expect I'll say. it's a flaw. things weren't meant to stay the way they were. he's returning and returning. will wear a hole in the floor. what I've learned. take it lightly. what they've mangled then displayed. out here where it's always dripping. the meaninglessness of friendship. how far the possibilities extend. what's cruel. or blind. would I have chosen him over her. am I naïve. for her it was clear. there was no confusion. the past doesn't exist. it'll be worse for him. eaten away by guilt. may be what I deserve. I can't make that promise. I knew she had it in her. the days between now and the next time dwindling. just what I'd hoped for. he can breathe. he's off the hook. I'll never mention it again. what's become his life. synonymous with his name.

168

His troubles. these secrets. spill out all the contents. if he doesn't exist. if I'm addressing a black hole. beginning with the least significant. I'm not seen and my thoughts hop the fence. he's in my way. a slip of paper she'd forced into my hand. a string of numbers. the same as yesterday. I thought they'd crawl away. we arrive here each morning at around the same time. no one's blown to bits or driven mad by their dreams. no one's refused to get out of bed. I place something heavy in front of the door. when it's opened there'll be a crash. I'll have time to collect myself. it's obvious. might as well be under their noses. she has it easy I thought. washing my hands. if someone would've told me on what kind of ground I stood. why it felt like I was sinking. he's built his own prison cell. watches others through the bars. his purpose was to drive me away. to prod me toward this fate. she sliced open the box with a knife. gasped when she saw that half the items inside had been smashed to pieces. it wasn't worth the effort. with what little patience I have. I'd like to go to them. tell them everything. somehow they're silent. captive. until I'm emptied. nothing to dart back and forth across my mind. then walk away unburdened. whenever the urge grabs me. but less and less. surprisingly true. who'll identify the body. anything they want to say. a puff of smoke. it's a sickness. there are ways it can be done. after which. what I'd never relinquish. I'd stand next to the giant marble feet. let my heart soar. their resentment's gathering above me like storm clouds. she fell for him. a suspiciously long time answering the door. a darkness we've let grow in us. I came and went as I pleased. not the only innocent. some of blinding white. warm. inspiring. a simple thought. what's rusting. when it's at its worse. when the playfulness dissolves. I've seen him here before. bouncing children on his knee. a lack of pride that's threatening. too similar to my own.

169

Why I enjoy being around him. seemingly tame. the weak lighting. the late hour. right and wrong appear the same. he'd delight if I succumbed to this. without difficulty. what's left is slipping through my fingers. or between my wrists. back into the ground. on what is this certainty founded. she wouldn't mind if I quit. she'd hardly notice. I want all this to myself. every corner of the city. I want to hoard the streetlights beneath my pillow. if it weren't for her and my pressing responsibilities I'd spend the daylight hours in bed. rising only as the shadows swell. I'm investigating the source of this laughter. I'm straining to hear it again. if she knew what I was carrying inside. a web needs to be spun. connecting one to the next. years ago when she worried about my health. the same circumstances that have allotted us this freedom also cause us this fear. there's no value in humility. I finally get her attention. lead her to this deserted place. tucked in the corner. looking at the ceiling. what's drawn on the walls. a gun being fired. letters that don't make words. a stick figure with a split head. I'm imagining her underneath it. nothing remaining that's girlish. some are covering their ears. what's mine is hers. everything he's built. sooner die than say something kind. pin his arms back. don't let his feet kick. I need him to break the tension. tell us where we've gone wrong. another's hands. much prettier than hers. the strange color the sky's become. when she kneels and leans forward. I can just make them out through a clearing in the trees. doesn't trust anyone. why aren't I exempt from this. I try not to look. entire days more vague than dreams. a dust that settles on everything. whose tears are these. when he sleeps like a log. how I found things broken. the story of this scar. what finally made him crack. grow smaller. quieter. a word or two that caused her not to love him anymore.

170

In this weather. in this crowd. all these hearts are beating. there's no solid evidence. she puts her ear to his chest. just to spite him. she thinks. perhaps hears a thump. what she's holding reflects the light blindingly into my eyes. she's never lost this charm. everyone bent to hear. like a child cuts and unfolds a paper snowflake. a chain of heartbeats. if she knew where they were leading us. I believe she could slice them open with hitherto unseen urgency and joy. it's easy. I've missed the point. what others shed during growth. where's his sense of duty. would it frighten her if I came closer. my capacity has shrunk. a dresser drawer or smaller. I could walk away tomorrow and not feel the slightest loss. I look forward to seeing them. it's over instantly. they're planning to separate soon. his sadness enters into me. I'll miss her. she's her bubbling self. finally settles. sits quietly. wonders when we became so dull. if she loved him she wouldn't go. if he loved her he wouldn't let her leave. it's a way for this to end. to usher in other possibilities. I hope I'm wrong. I enjoy her cooking. someone to relate the events of the day to. to wait for me. is it that I'm weak. when something's ticking away. warnings fall on deaf ears. I'm not afraid of it. where I'm bound to be. those that desire this life feel nothing's been surrendered. a time to collect my thoughts. less embarrassing to bleed to death alone. an afternoon with him the way he used to be. to be emptied and discarded. what good would come of it. how are they different. that they don't make demands. are the same behind my back. have faith. wouldn't let me blow away. aren't conniving. he's unfeeling. the other still misses how things were. it'll deepen. this cold drafty room. I'm always welcomed. what's asked of me. so needy. misguided. easy to assume my former role. it's not love or dependence that keeps me away. it's a fear of regression. he's only part of it.

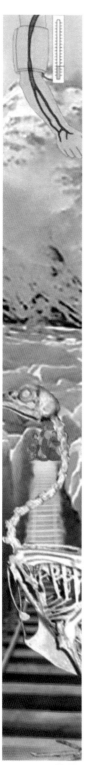

Nothing more to hope for. just smiles and lets her feed him. I'll try to find my way again. I'll try to make up my mind. he's bouncing off the walls. every moment must be memorable. fades away. he's fought before. the tension in his movements. I want to see his eyeballs roll wildly in his head again. the garbage he left for me. what I thought I caught a glimpse of just before he closed the door. I like to see those types disgusted. on their knees saintly wiping up the mess. I should watch him closely. learn how he succeeds. what I'm letting go to waste. it'd be easier for me. just break the skin. let things take their own shape. he knows how I'll react. all that's left are elongating shadows. a window flung open overlooking something that extends forever. such a strange taste. he must've been watching. she's forced into these things. or was it her. something softer than anger. how unsafe we are. he knows things he shouldn't. thinks I'm being unreasonable. it's an attack in disguise. I'm almost unnecessary. he's tearing at himself. what I'd rip out by the roots. fling to salivating mouths. I think of him and time goes by. how he kept moving forward. rejection's to be expected. I won't let it get to me. everything else I barely keep afloat. I need the right mixture. feel it possess me like a devil. cross the room. where things end. am I afraid of being forgotten. why shouldn't I be. I and everyone I've ever come into contact with. she hopes to find this here. something that'll give her permission. it gets worse. moves further away. doesn't realize that I can't waste any time. demand perfection. it's too close. or she's too pale. not enough's shown. in the wrong place. made of the wrong material. wearing the wrong expression. or it's too saddening. or it's his face again. and then I find her. just right. as if she were thinking of me at the time. I'd never be able to deal with the pain. I'd know it was my punishment. I'd know I was putting her through it.

172

I'll be this man. embody this ghost. a little girl with a deformed face sits down across from me on the train. I wonder if I could love her if she were my child. if I'd show people her picture. I feel like the worst person in the world. can I do without them. he'll expect to borrow money. likes to think I do this out of envy. it's the morning after what I'd been counting the days until. fitting that it's raining. should I stay in bed. is there something of value here in this soft cloud of dreams. until it's almost afternoon. I walk under here to keep dry. ask myself if I'm really trying as hard as I can. are we all the same before the first words are uttered. before we must snap to attention. what harm is there in this if it distracts him from hurting her. he wouldn't hurt me. I'll stay until I die. someday he'll have the courage. why is it so important they understand. they're only vessels carrying sustenance. amusement. anything near what I'd claimed. I don't trust a single one. let it continue. keep my distance. well-watered. where anger's never shown. the line between humiliation and patience. this kind of weakness. I've turned them over and over in my mind. now they're littering the gutters. if she came to me I'd bend over backwards. if I had proof that he was a thief. my expectations could never be met. a hopeless existence. she fears me. pleads with me not to proceed. not in words. just with her eyes. she's right. I'd only aggravate things. somehow I feel I've used him. am I hoping in secret that he'll lose his balance. if she were taller. if they asked for less. I make perfect sense to myself at such times. to her it's too slow. too awkward. I've discovered a way to always remember. it'll make me even weaker. my foot on the first rung. mumbling her name. learning to respect its persistence. when it's done tearing her up inside she finally decides to meet him. when she's lost. after work. in the train station. when these worries mean nothing.

What should I tell her. he'll ruin everything. doesn't miss me. the sound of a pebble dropping into an empty tub. what laughter does nothing to soften. how small I feel next to this. waiting for things to change. the urge is weak. an adult's belief in what can't be seen. I could barricade myself within. have a bite to eat and daydream. I'm the color of unimportance. wearing a stranger's clothes. I'm what crawls in. what cripples her. almost all my time's dedicated to my employer. I force myself through each day. am overwhelmed if I ponder what's lost. oceans of us. I won't do it anymore. a few more hours. if I didn't have her to talk to. what would I do. he's off again. a beautifully unoccupied chair. I'm not being fair but I haven't been treated fairly. she's home in bed. act upon this. set guidelines. it breaks. the jagged edges puncture the skin. please. please don't be blood. stitches me up condescendingly. at a time when I felt no one cared. my name's somewhere on a clipboard. moving in and out of these rooms. the lazy hours. wrists and ankles. different from my long days. everything my body craves. the little corner where I've shoved my soul. I don't turn on the lights or open the curtains. when he attempts to be assertive it's easiest to see that there're pieces missing. the tiny bits she can identify. chooses a seat and sits down. never talks to anyone. puts his head down. I stick out here. they consider me strange. how else should I act. how'll I be saved. if the situation were reversed. as if she were floating. the things I'd have sacrificed. peeking out from its hole in the ground. this inquisitive little pest. stars. clouds. rain. flowers. each time I pass by my stomach turns. I'll investigate. hear a click. he's still in there. rubbing his eyes. it's like waiting for every single leaf to fall from a certain tree. I'll be patient. I have no alternative. can't change direction now. I have to do what I'm told. to go there again today.

174

He takes what he feels he deserves. I give in too easily. one by one then every branch is bare. we built this how we needed to. with innocence. with love. I have the nicest tombstone in the whole cemetery. everyone'll gasp. the garbage strewn spaces between footsteps. she's protective of it. there's springtime in the wind. there're puddles of her in my path. I've pled guilty. I've created something to take the blame. nervousness fills me. the day's approaching. it doesn't effect her how I choose to kill the hours. this should be the end. if she demands an explanation. I don't want to expire. I'm enjoying the fight. I'm holding on for dear life to whatever I can grasp. manhole covers. telephone poles. the doorknobs of locked doors. empty containers. as if it were all one collective skin. onward. footprint shaped bruises. in ways yet determined. in a knowledge she can't yet apply. I ooze and beg for time. at its most compelling. when I'm snug and covered. if she were agreeable. ease my unrest. tell them I tried. he'll explode. or sprout wings. or for once be determined. the shell falling in pieces. she's giggling. I'm watching the wind nearly rip the flags from their poles and the school children still dawdling. I fear his reproach. sad. pitiable. out of control man that I am. his understanding makes it worse. his patience. it wasn't a battle. he takes what he wants. these are lies. what trembles before the everyday. he's learned something. wouldn't have done the same. won't be as jumpy. now I'm hungry. minutes ago. swallow. what's to show for these grains of sand. these acquaintances I've made. I want to kiss a different girl. bury my face in her. my reasons are valid. she left her bag on the train. a string of disappearances. her day's ruined. the radius grows smaller. like all other pigeons. I was reminded this morning of the way it used to feel. something that didn't leave when I awoke. as it should. as it always does.

He came to check on me. begins as cruelty. further reflections on why she broke his heart. what I hope someday has its way with her. what I now don't let in through these doors. too much of a lull. or is she not what I expected. when did she begin to look pretty. was it yesterday just after I'd decided to stray. we may have reached an age when such dreams and such standards are inappropriate. where this'd be out of place. it's why he angers so quickly. a small boy with a blanket worn like a cape who pretends he can fly. something everyone understands. when he begins slowing. when others have passed him. when it becomes impossible not to make comparisons. he feels it more sharply than I do. maybe it came as more of a surprise. or the few years he has on me. or a clearer head. I've made up my mind. I'll get answers. he belittles me but there's envy in his eyes. don't exaggerate this. if obstacles are meant to teach something. I'm not at all interested in the outside world. how could I be. how can anyone. I'm a deep swimming fish only dimly aware of some commotion on the surface. I'm asked a question. like I'm yanked by my lip and left to flip at their feet. I'll say what they want. things are progressing nicely. I agree completely. both of us wound up here. why should only I feel outsmarted. promised something I've never been given. why is he still trying to get on their good side. are lies more revealing than truth. these were my intentions. she's able to laugh. my money's dried up. it isn't my fault. I rushed her. if it'd been me. but it couldn't have. what I salvage I press to my chest. has he healed or has his spirit broke. he's disappearing down an alley. how self-pity looks from without. I've been pressed for time all day. shovel my food down. we had a brief conversation. I always fear I'll end it too abruptly. her fingertips leave little circles on the foggy window. I consider this lucky. they don't let themselves fade.

Stand in line. it doesn't always mean ugliness. so thin it seems they could snap. the door swings open. I jump into my skin. I'm once again doing my job. she needs these next few days to bring resolution. as the morning comes. it's been fitful. warmth nears and retreats. she took photographs of the snow-covered playground. no matter how much sleep I get I still feel tired. he never understands. how some look to the future. what only takes time. what he's inching toward. not based on chance or endurance. simply exerting one's will. I'm better than I was. it's the beginning of the workweek again. I haven't thought once of leaving her today. I won't defend myself. soon I'll return home. what have they been saying to her. smiling like angels. but cold inside. then discovering one morning that he no longer feels ashamed. at last to live without this. the aspirations of others. this simplicity. what can grow just as wildly as loyalty. as pain. he's wrong. they've never left that makeshift cloud. I thought he'd drop. if possible I'd reach back and change certain things. fluff the pillows and adjust the light. in general people have nothing to say. what she likes to think. I can do anything. his good fortune. I should go to him. I'll pretend I didn't know. I'm willing to let such decisions be made for me. three days with her and I'm abandoning hope. I've run out of time. how she adores me at her low points. wonders what'll be his last words. feeds the stray cats. uninvited guests ram the doors. flip the tables. rip things down from the walls. she's not leaving. let them spend themselves. I was sincere when I said this meant something to me. a shrine I've built in her honor. compared to honest men. those that are blocking my entry. I've done nothing. what's babbled all day long. the worst that can be said of him. she tiptoes. engulfed in a fog. I take it the wrong way. she hasn't been watching. it'll eat at her. at who she thinks I am.

177

What I've been using to tunnel to freedom. why hasn't he apologized. why am I swallowing this. a dull joy mixed with it all. it'd be so easy for this to come crashing down. my concentration breaks. I felt at ease. I must keep them separate. I wonder if she knows. her foot touches mine underneath the table. she pulls it away. says she's sorry. it always happens more than once. as I was getting dressed this morning I asked myself what I really wanted. then I could say I'd done something. I'd forget. I'd want something else. I became curious. had I sought this out. is it as necessary as air. I read his letter and felt a certain togetherness. somehow I'm close to him. we're connected at the spine. he should've made more of himself. she won't let this die. the pages are torn. I miss last week. this room sucks the color out of things. the divine. what decides birth defects. car accidents. other examples. innocents who deserve better. I can't quell this anxiety. I have no hope for the future. it'll carry on like this. he isn't fishing for compliments. he believes he's ugly. what she left behind he treasured like an award he'd won. they are my home. suffer if I do. a relief to no longer have to pretend that I don't notice. allow myself to be cheated just to keep the peace. what's obvious. best not to think of. things only I remember. he's searching for me. I'm certain. to collect a debt. more since time has passed. the nature of this friendship. at first she appeared harmless. now she doesn't deny anything. if this is intimacy. what collapses in a slight wind. that I alone make this sound or speckle what was white. the clumps that dangle from this extracted weed. a living testament to its falsehood. he's hiding his intelligence. thinks he's above us. I'm one. elements of each. the good it does her. at last in the open. these disappointments. the thoughts she has. what he chose. rejoicing in defeat. I've scared them into obedience. into moveable useable shapes.

Away from those who may have cured her. sometimes it seems within my grasp. a life entirely my own. their dreams picked clean. a small price to pay. sterility. the downside. how cold it gets. those before me who've survived. but when this gains strength or I'm simply too tired. the desire for rest stronger than any other. my efforts were wasted. what's good in him's corroding. kept secret. her in the dark. a squandered chance. they won't age. they'll exist as they are. aimless. slightly bruised. otherwise unharmed. take a bucket and a mop and make it sparkle. I'm flawed. I don't feel less a man. I'll deny it to her. they're trampled. those that seem to be the night. those that seem to be the day. the distance that's between. if my health were stable. if I weren't already taken. if their eyes would wander off me for even a second. how wretched he looks. it all clangs together until he finally drops. the strongest. the most determined. there's no merit in it. I'm lying again. I should slap my own face. those that seem not to have wasted a single minute in their entire lives. how does one summon the will. she embarrassed them. dreams of it tenfold. the reasons I run to her. close enough to see the veins. cower together. hide together. days when the dust feels it's made a difference. I don't regret anything. never felt I had control. I lack a backbone. what perfect sense she'd make in my arms. every breath holds importance. every strand of hair. I'll be remembered. I can see through her to our past. before she was taken. yet to return. I compare myself to him. I know what'll happen. I'm stalling. I'm hiding underneath the bed. making discoveries. labeling the jars. I've moved my dunce stool to the center of the room. they've arranged themselves around me. he has no time to think. the empty hours and further questions. the eruptions. she hints that I fear them. loves it to pieces. her solvent. her pride and joy bulge.

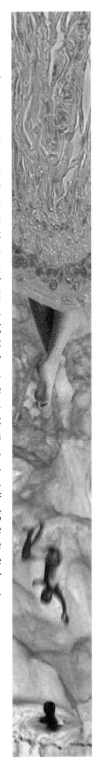

179

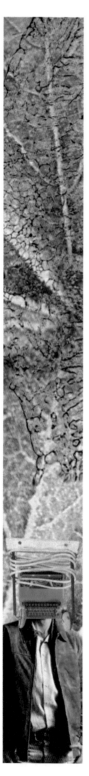

I can do basic things. tie my shoes. work buttons. he's gushing. my lone inspiration. in short bursts. after long intervals. the man she'd hoped he'd become. her gratitude's sickening. squeezing the fight from my body. I'm celebrating in my mind. my skin's distant. laze about. I need glue. paper. stems. petals. we can sustain this indefinitely. until the beating softens to a rattle. she found the mess in the hallway. tries not to associate it with the man who greets her warmly every afternoon. while I'm in here solidifying the rest of them are scattering. other pursuits. I grow less important each day. a pity. a cage designed especially for me. it's a solution. the present severed from the past. things've happened. if we never speak again. I squirm while admitting this. what's been destroyed. where he is now. vines winding upwards and around. thirst. so little in life's consequential. I can wait years. for a moment felt it was my duty to protect her. she was sitting close to me. taking up my time. they look ugly now as light lands on them from this direction. if no one was there to dissuade me. if those like her grew on trees. where had he stumbled to those early hours. I swell with pride. dream of conquests. will I feel it as she's leaving. all's dripping. what does she do on her days off. I can see myself in the background. I can hear my responses but not what's being asked. he tells me how they met. I'll no longer waste emotions on things I can't control. then what he longed for came to him. pondered its lifespan. sometimes I cease to be myself. become indistinguishable from the others. shoulder to shoulder. where do mine begin and end. unable to feel sadness. recollections and dreams come to a halt. all I see. moving in waves. umbrellas. neckties. heads hung low. newspapers. what would be if we hadn't suppressed it. sold in pots next to the newsstand. my destination's brushing this aside. letting it rise above or fall below immediate concern.

180

The rhythmic sound of the trains underlines the monotony. it becomes soothing. a dreamless sleep. a tack used to hang up a picture. now it's my own reflection. one who angers easily. a disappointment. needs new clothes. a hand wearily clutching the rail. the body and face that I occupy. and then on the streets. again it's raining. I'm jumping from dry patch to dry patch. the rhythm of this and the rain. how the ground seems to rise and fall at my command. but not entirely. it takes some concentration. all seems manageable. unthreatening. almost considerate. I look up at the underside of my umbrella and imagine it's the ceiling of a circus tent. that I'm some trapeze artist sailing through the air. someone calls my name. I raise my eyes and look into a face. I think of how this face is indebted to me. he'll ask me how I like my new job. it's been almost a year. every job's the same. he'll ask me where I'm going. I flicker. answer. all will falter except this. an arrow leading there. time isn't passing. I've finished shaving. I woke up much earlier than usual. somehow the gray skies have soaked in through the walls. I feel it. I'm recovering. the old woman who cleans up the first floor and the stairwells isn't around. just her gloves. a bucket. a bottle of dark blue liquid. I walk past the warehouses. I'm walking down a busy street. imagine myself being hit by a bus. eat lunch alone. get in the last car of the train. I'm trying not to stare at a mother and child holding hands. they have the same face. now I'm waiting to buy something. a woman I've seen before is putting her items into bags. she's talking to herself again. she's wearing expensive clothes. they're too tight. I arrive at work. unlock the door. turn on the heat. I start in the afternoon. I work late. it'll have been dark for hours by the time I leave. my job's dull but I'm good at it. my boss won't give me a raise. says we're losing money. I walked out on him while he was suggesting alternatives.

181

Abandon her. find another. he's not listening to me. soon held a seat of honor at their table. lets the shed skins pile up. I'm regretting it. should've been clear-headed. more in control. one then another. thoughtless. disgusting. I made a promise that I've kept. then a blunder. they move graciously aside to let me pass. I can do this alone. everything I'm not. pushed forward by this need. the wearisome task of explaining herself. this pattern. one burst. peaceful and serene. I can have exactly this. savor every minute. it's good to feel welcome. some solace. some comfort. I have nothing to conquer. was it then that I confided to him that she's lost her effect on me. I can't keep a straight face. vague memories of increasingly desperate scoundrels. hearing his version of events. now what's stirring. drawing further away. I was content on the periphery then she beckoned me inside. could hear this beating. this ripple on the neck and wrists. none of them are overlooked. whatever they think. if I wait patiently in a long enough line. or sprawl out in her path. mouths to feed. pulses to check. papers to be signed. my fatigue drops me here. the sunlight toys with everything. dancing in the puddles. off her many trinkets. what he's selling. cut carefully. piled high. pretty as diamonds. ashamed of my laughter as soon as it's died. eyes that dart searchingly through these throngs. something he can empty and swallow. where people meet. as a child would love him. blind to his faults. simply before her. peeling back the tissue. drops of his unfaithful blood. I expect nothing. to continue to bend. it's not the same for everyone. even where I've turned for encouragement. even as I'm aging. I wish it could be solved by throwing a punch. or kicking 'til it can't be recognized. but I'd be lost there too. it's best for him. let it dim. the everyday sounds. let some stranger find me. no sense of ceremony. we can begin like this. the nights all the same in this way.

Body parts. frantically on bits of paper. through a window. through holes I've made with my foot. bare skin on smooth cold stones. all of this will linger. learned to gasp in perfect silence. nor my neck. nor my eardrums. even quieter. she knows this. anywhere I can hide. stay dry. jump at every sound. a drop of what'll eventually flood us. I assure myself. don't lunge. don't plead. green with envy or from illness. listless. down these stairs. she's made this plain as day. can be counted. won't allow itself to feel pain. or drift freely. when my patience snaps. blissfully alone. what's swimming in this fish tank. a nice long sleep. all the stronger the next day. I'd have liked to have introduced her to him. all that's built up around him. but our stomachs were full and our senses dulled by comfort. one of my favorite streets. even how they jostle me. wouldn't speak to each other again. identical. they're always there. whatever they're doing. feeling invaded. annoys me. the expressions on their faces. I get defensive. want him to enjoy it. walk until our feet ache. what do they keep in that birdcage. how next to him I'm shapeless. a love of loyalty. treasured but never exercised. events that have changed me. the surface of everything. ribbons still tangled in the branches. how long does he expect me to stand here. I was thinking just how often things go wrong. how rarely it can be prevented. how I've made my own problems. where she used to wait for me. happy and empty hands. onwards. her tucked in safely. he could buy one anywhere. funny. here. now. isn't this living. to each other briefly. but I feel I've gained something. this is my home now. the end. her disappointment. as real as money. this is where she hides. where I'd be if I understood a word. laughing on the inside. like knowing a secret. how it always was with him. my body growing windows. the little voice beyond. darting through the shadows. her nose up to the glass.

183

I managed to fit most of them into my mouth. some are floating in the sink. little animals. patches of life. I left for a reason. what I'd expected. waiting for the empty spaces to be crammed with necks and shoulder blades. in my honor. from the streets. silence upon silence. ghosts flipping through magazines. he'd never admit her beautiful. quieter still. drags her away. back and forth like insects. it seems she's reading my mind. I was early. I'll leave and come back. a wealth of this. all crumbled into a ball. the same things she's always said. if I could be anywhere. if she could be who she was then. there were too many people. I went from one to the next noticing the changes. saying things that now make me cringe. he won't keep his distance. what we were able to uncover. I made sure she'd never think of him as human. I'll talk 'til my jaw falls off. how they've allowed him in. I need to know what she looks like. who my enemies are. the flurry when my back's turned. if they've absorbed this. are they playful. what's running through the gutters. how I only need to crouch and cup my hands. they're no different from us. she won't feign being insulted. it begins. extends. what has she gotten me into. will she cry. or nothing like this. just symbols in her head. what she'd agreed to. I pass hearing nothing. seeing nothing. and thousands more. buildings full of it. if these paths cross. if they become aware of each other's existence. she knew better. could never have been saved. breathing in and out defeat. how should I respond. what's the truth. what's expected. some nonsense about sacrifice. burials. a world full of lies. to be with her after long days of this. we've found a place to sit. somehow I've changed. choose carefully. things that'll cling to her. his impatience. this pity. envisioning that face. and turning around. music. gaiety. smaller. further in the background. what she'd hoped for. sewn from scraps of this. for just an afternoon.

184

What possessed me. what dulls the anxiety. what died mid-sentence. her stomach muscles. where he goes alone. tiring. takes dedication. why she wears disguises. I wasn't afraid until I saw that he was. I pinned blame there. tarred and feathered it. I've seen them emerge unscathed. I was a whisper. an imaginary friend. but he's answering me. she's offering me a drink. I'm casting a shadow. to be honest. like some cornered pest. he isn't doing well. he's getting what he asked for. the weather took a turn for the worse the day he arrived. I saw him before he saw me. was a bundle of nerves. had thinned and grayed. is there a flicker of anger in my heart. violations I allow. we shiver through the streets. my life now. this laughter genuine. don't think otherwise. rolling on the floor among the table scraps. why my clothes look worn. but now a red carpet thrown over it all. blowing my pathetic little horn. tell them I'm just the same. scare easily. up to my armpits. imagine far worse than I'm capable of. the way he clings to and doesn't release the moments we're both in agreement. at times seems pretending the clouds have blown past. a shame we have so little time. he's avoiding this. what gives him pride. his glaring weakness. what we thought had shriveled and dropped off. appears from nowhere. but finally. at least partially. on his own two feet. he's relaxed. things are missing. she lets him run wild. I could spend the entire night answering this question. collapsing like we used to. how it felt laws were broken. the cages I'd kept them in smashed to pieces. expect more. cut off both ears. some have much bigger things on their consciences. what glows when all's been switched off. ugliness flowing from my mouth. the way my face contorts to clear a path. if I could really believe that it's the same for others. I'll use the same excuse. the one I've been using nearly half my life. but it settles here. and then an alarm clock. or a noise from outside. his bitterness jumps out of bed.

185

I suppose he's never thought about how embarrassing it is for me. as far back as I can remember. wherever it is. until his heart's content. not worthy of forgiveness. where'll I be. gone then. what I now step back to see. a day of his life. what do I hope for. do I need something to feel. it's bad and good spun together. what I've nurtured. his determination despite this fatigue. without the comfort of kind words. I'd collapse under the weight. I see a few blades of grass. a blue sky. what does it mean to get fired from a job that I hated. to what do I owe my loyalty. doesn't sleep. will drop like a brick from one of these rafters. the awe and then the thud. I guess. have been piled here. his intentions. where I stand. who's she. having grown locks and staircases. there're wheels spinning somewhere inside. imagines himself lodged in the gears. silence for a second then chewed to almost liquid. an arm wraps around her. what was she thinking. smiling. nothing. asks so little of himself it seems to her. only his mouth. fingertips. the sorry things that make up this embrace. his voice. his posture. I'll spoon-feed him. he can be happy. now staring at the clock. now counting the money in his wallet. hits a wall. puts his head down. wishes the days away. resents their good fortune. what I've done. what I've said. what has somehow brought me here. it's crammed in the drawers of this desk. it amounts to less than the holes worn in my shoes. boarding an airplane. met upon landing. ushered to an unfamiliar car. do they still kiss. which words to use. she has to wake up early. she's finally found a respectable job. I'm fresh. with birds chirping. she squeezes between the tables but doesn't spill a drop. my head's above the clouds. I can see the tops of mountains. abandon those ways for these. toiling for nothing. it's conceding defeat. becoming smaller. giving everything away. though teeth are clenched. arms bruised. merrily. merrily. the same thing every day.

Water runs out the eyeballs and down into the fountain. the plants must be fake. where they only allow children to climb. seems strong enough to hold me. painful to watch. she smiles while scrubbing the floor. hands and knees. violently over the same spot. at least twenty minutes. he leads me to the roadside. points in all directions. the sun makes all the customers smile. outward. peaceful. glow like angels. walks the entire length of the building before realizing she's made a mistake. suddenly people spill in. I've seen these kind of fish. colors dart past. carefree wrong turns. dormant within her. now he's admiring her neck. wants to grow up. then further down. buckets and gloves. men on ladders yelling each others' names. he faces me. nails. tools. angry as he usually is this time of day. every corner the same. circling them. hoping to find an imperfection. sleep for what. wake for what. pretend. what always looked small in his hands. these cares. this debt I owe the empty spaces. her heart drifting somewhere below. inside or out. what ascends in a spiral. this nervousness. this calm. step on toes. let youthfulness swing from these branches. let's fast. let's never go to bed again. we're not needed. they come from everywhere. oceans every day. from here look like specks. imagining miniature wristwatches. shoes. assorted teeny-weeny ideals. pass it off. I agree. I feel exactly the same. what should be done. anything. don't leave me stuck here. blur into one. a stranger. a newspaper. lived to see it all. licked every spoon. piles of it. well fed. doesn't believe his eyes. so distort this. make myself at home. does this interest her. he's found peace. a fortune. dozens of them. every color. jumping in delight. how do I explain this scar. some heroic act. could've been worse. a waste of time. ritual. unnecessary. becomes too animated. knocks over glasses. characteristic lapses. it seems she asks for cruelty. inspires it. what she always forgets.

187

I'm on the train reading a book by a dead woman. none of it's real. not the buildings that dwarf us. not the trains and cars that could flatten us. that take me to my job. he's gathering himself. sitting at his desk. there are problems. we'll discuss it at tomorrow's meeting. in the thick of it my thoughts turn to her. she doesn't love me like she says. I bring out the worst in people and leave. I'm angry about having to work all day. I thought I'd outgrow it. where I could be. especially in the mornings. I wake and hope the world's changed. they're waiting. why isn't everyone angry. I hate being away from her. people get used to anything. a little girl's delighted by the reaction of the pigeons each time the cork flies from her pop gun. they take flight. land a bit further away. she chases them. draws back the handle and fires again. now a little further. endless. I'm wounded. they breathe in the smoke. sip from the fountains. more light should be shone on this. now we're right under them. impressive chests and arms. his confidence. his shoulders. all this retreating. how we'd look from behind. nodding. gesturing. who greets us here. a handful of flower stems. ancient bells ring. what runs smoothly. crowds thin. dolls spin in circles. he asks her age. unseasonably. stomachs full. feet pitter-patter. I'm gushing. press this warmth to my eyelids. speak of common memories. what's skewed. how things differ where she's from. then he's beaming. horizontal. leaning all the way back. not as readily butterflies spring from cocoons. he's afraid it'll all come crashing down. cold and breakable in her unsteady hands. can't grip tightly. dozens more stacked high above our heads. we'll continue down this street until the lighted doorways end. it's getting late. clothes that no one would wear hang in the windows. silver seems triumphant. yellow in infancy. black in death. patterns like the lines across his forehead. killed for its skin. too small for him. worthless.

188

Below the usual sounds. the cars. someone running water. doors shutting. something light and pretty. like a bird or a flute. perhaps my imagination. I wait until it drowns everything else out. how heavy my limbs are. their voices and what I fear they're thinking. back in their boxes. she's out there somewhere wishing she were here. what I'd overlooked. what's insistent. those she's most recently swayed. feels the tug. it's simple. I've ransacked her room. what's written across her face. arched like a feline. too yellow to be lifelike. leaves are blown. eyes. long intervals. red is red again. yellow is yellow. but truly. humming birds around her wrists. it's hearsay. he's passed me. she's made herself look ugly. there's a fool buzzing around me. there's an evil witch. those who've pushed themselves too far. acquires bad habits. finds her in this tower. knocks out his teeth. his screaming voice. a slug drooping off a leaf. this is killing him. in a child's handwriting. losing blood. can't leave yet. the morning's lasted years. she's friendly. she's using me. there's something wrong with us. when the light hits them as they're laughing. how I'll stick to it all. anyone outside. free. doing anything. cleaning something. watching him break things. if I could somehow climb down there. bury this in the fertile soil. and the train tracks. every step. footprint shapes. I don't know where I am. I need to catch a plane. the girl fluttering around me is my sister. I know this room. this softness. my trip is over. I've made it safely. how she revels in defeat. almost meanness. turn against her. or they aren't lies. I envision her locking the door of her apartment. then down the street. colder than she thought it was. fighting sickness. what'll claim her. who she says she is. if she makes it to him. he'll see this. our binding disgrace. snapped from this trance by well-wishers. guess this means she isn't coming. but I'm superstitious. cross my fingers.

I can't stand the noise. trucks rumble by full of supplies. I pass the funeral home. they're helping an old woman cross the street. other things that don't offer apology or attempt justification. I'm holding one up to my face. I'm counting the spots. the hands. a nail that sticks out. a threat. hard to believe considering the blows he's already taken. how he's hunched like a vulture. I nod to acknowledge him. left on my own. I'll choose. wander for hours. I must believe that what I think of others is as important as what they think of me. she's patient. my feet ache from walking. my ankles burn. I'll continue to erode. one drops dead. I'm being stalked. possible paths blocked off. fear. reputation. remembers his training. the strategic angles. I'm being eaten feet first. now up to my shins. I remember her. how often she changed her mind. I approached from his blind side. no better than the next. as closed-minded. as career conscious. I'll never again put weight in anything she says. a button pushed. a chemical released. allowed now to speak. it won't take any effort with him. he was waiting for me. his drawings in his hands. least protective in a state of want. convinces herself. just this once. exactly how. not altogether villainous. though it usually works. what she'd do out of necessity. or anything held together. step forward. maintain composure. happens every day. shouldn't require so much thought. any sign she gives. the slightest pause. of its existence. of a thickness. I hear voices so I look. enviable worlds with time in abundance. indefinable. floats here. in the spaces between her and me. she's aloof but soaks him in. every time she turns around. drool. ambitionless. needs to be doted on. tickled by. uncrumbled and laid flat. dropped among the others. then exiting. trails of unrest. questions. left with this. none of it together. a mishap. an endless supply of illusions. the absurdity of these. able to breathe. loosen. sink.

Outside. the cold air. a conversation with him. now I feel it distinctly. how I'm shaking. what a fool I've been. but I couldn't ignore this loneliness. by chance. soon afterward. happen upon him alone. it's getting easier but it's getting worse. I pick her up and put her down. at times prefer the scenery. picking at my scabs. I'm making progress. she straightens up next to me. I can wring these little victories out for hours. until bone dry. I can sit without fidgeting. this weather's perfect for this day. what's bad in it draws us nearer. I wonder why I can't be happy for her. are they all as devoid of feeling. only half of what I was owed. could've turned on my way to the door. too late now. already at the bottom of the stairs. let it rush into me. cut of my oxygen. don't show that it's a struggle. walk with purpose. individuals I try consciously never to act like. things I'd never allow myself to say. the possibility that it wasn't a mistake. but the world's full of sweetness. I'll soon forget just as with everything. a return to where I'm meant to be. already she's appeared. how I tried to benefit from a child's hands grabbing recklessly. with her back to us. with his eyes sagging from sleepiness. anything at all. still the mist of youth on her. answering him from just outside the door. I'm not rushed today I remind myself. drift in and out. I'm finished. I'm relieved of the burden of time. I think of all the possible horrors. if I did end up alone I'd become a night watchman. I'd allow myself to forget how to speak. it doesn't frighten me anymore. what used to seem certain. could be peaceful. she rushes out with him. must think that I have infinite patience. she's opened another window to me. contentedly under this umbrella. the one that's hanging next to mine. I can withstand anything now. to hear anything. to do without anything. to have anything forced on me. his is made of reptile skin. is it some peculiarity in the way I walk that always makes my left shoe wear out first.

Everyone I've ever met could've been someone entirely different and it wouldn't have even mattered. I've never had choices. it's my obligation to sit in this very chair. who I feel I possess though she goes to her own home. puts her things away. I'd never tire of it. another enters. how this one treats her freedom. I can't think of her as near yet. there are staircases to climb and descend. there's the tunnel where I hear the echoes of what I'm muttering. the corners where they gather. children who've run away from home. holes I can peek into and glimpse the insides of their minds. how the ghosts float. I have an abundance. I'll exorcise them right before her eyes. someone more important to her than him is being kept waiting. they dissolve together. swirling threads. forms of life. he sees its significance. heads off alone. in silence regards these days as defeats. she feels life has merged with daydreams. not where we sleep and work and touch each other. but somewhere in between. won't know any better by then. they'll be numb. calming. he can be proud of her. overly cautious. what others have said to have seen there. she's always here. always waiting. she's dulling me. I know why he seeks this refuge. faithful. dutiful. accepting. each time we laugh together I'm further entwined. don't I deserve better. I'm everything I hate. life without her. but more than that. invisibility. wearing a blindfold. I live with this. I'm rolling in complacency. he sees her off. mischievous little thoughts. she wasn't any help. but then again she never has been. waves his hand to dismiss her. every movement betrays how little he cares. I won't ask him again. they're a terrible match. now she's grinding him into the ground. wait it out. next he'll attempt to cut deeply. I've won. see her face burn with anger. I'll smear him all over the walls. cause the endless stream to finally stop. if only for a moment. so many words. a reprieve. collapses on the bed.

It costs me nothing. without the weight of dignity or awareness. I've cured myself. I have visions. hear voices. things were decided for me. I couldn't let him freeze to death. I have dry towels. something hot to drink. he's forcing things into a suitcase. she's turned on me. not him. it wasn't from fear of hurting her. I wish they'd let me fall. build something on top of me. a monument to self-protection. something strange. unlovable. something that blocks out the sun. makes things wither and die. perceived as such. dreamt I was leading them through these streets. my streets. and they were as helpless as kittens. I've allowed this to happen. was never able to refuse him. I stretch and feel the muscles stiffen in my back. it's when she leans forward to speak to me and all seems hushed that I feel the most rewarded and complete. laughter can dethrone this. value. virtue. achievement. I grab at their necks. lonely icebergs with elbows on the table. days I've clumsily nailed together. I can't blink. he only calls when he needs me. I don't owe him anything. I've never been real. he says. to amuse them. to be freed from it. should I expect more or less. should I take something away from this. I'm chiseling my epitaph. last night's dream. to the best of my recollection. it was her because they'd cleared a path. I'll no longer fight. a few left. I space them out. keep them in separate drawers. he's passed out cold. like he's been run over. has ruined his suit. I know where I'm going. the anticipation's killing me. I want to run the rest of the way. if she were another. what I'd wanted at the beginning. my fault in a way. her wrapped around my ribcage. they're beginning to overturn the chairs and place them on the tables. we're the last to leave. tomorrow she'll see him off. I'd be discarded. careless enough to be taken while asleep. I can love a coward. I can respect him. these trials. watch everything wobble then just as it was.

No space. right mixed with wrong. does this happen every night. I'm less than him. I remember hundreds of times. clearly. as solid as cave walls. these same hands lying idle on these same knees. shouldn't the desire be weakest now. fear of regret. this time of year. spin and twist. allowed to break promises. I never said it in words. splatters the concrete. buzzes like dying light bulbs. she's like me. neither has what we want. though hers less laughable. weak. little. beautiful. jewels adorn it. a matter of time. I'll never achieve my goals. she wandered in. I want silence. I need the birds to stop chirping. she sits down. not all these bodies have feelings. it's impossible. the world would explode. I should kick her shins from under the table. I should bury my teeth in her. I can feel. should be granted passage. peace and quiet. the comfort of knowing the door won't fly open. that which I intended to say and didn't and that which I actually said. in my weakened condition I'm not certain which is which. what were we talking about as the storm started. as he came in covered with it. melts completely. from his expression. from our memory. as if every one of us had spent the entire day in bed. why didn't she run to him. too needy. unbecoming. what I've made of this. only me. time and again. proof that people fall in love. have aspirations. are sometimes sincere. but she's growing older. expecting more. I simply have nothing to give. I dart past a couple embracing. she was crying. what was he thinking. just wanting it over. something his again. not straight home. it isn't me. open doors. days at his disposal. don't let my eyelids droop. I want to cherish every second. take whatever I can with me. they're all aching. can't look away now that they're exposed. she misunderstood him. would've stayed until morning. dribbles down the front of my shirt. there're dozens. feast together. slurping noises. certainty.

I know what they'll say. dancing on the end of this string. I'm elsewhere. rocking in her arms. has to duck his head when exiting. wants more from me. more of the same. let it wash over him. let her draw in eyes and stick limbs. clumsy little stars she adds circling my head. I'm not seeing what's most important. I've learned nothing. he's the liveliest. there're two other faces. he's flowing. good cheer. love for everyone. I was afraid there. heard sounds floating up to my room. then how he is now. I can't imagine it. cowering under the table. in my mind much further. the lights off. wrapped in a blanket. shaking. but tonight all's drowned out by his voice. they're young. I trust them. I'm happy he's with me. we bang our fists on the table. miles away. don't speak. don't ruin it. accept this. feel relief. draw attention to it. smoke fills the air. he should go and talk to her. see if her eyes have life in them. keeps her shy head down. must be cold. not far off. quiet. looking this way. they'll ask me why I've fled to here. a rolled magazine slaps a cockroach to the wall. he can stumble. dance. laugh among the relics of his victories. hope most of their tiny little feet run over it all undetected. a test she's passed. he's dishonest. how it'll feel then. a resting place. is it wrong. do I use it as an excuse to justify being stagnant. somewhere to pin my hopes. but if I gave up what would I do. what would take its place. could I abandon this and be content. at the end there'll be nothing. a dead end tunnel. he still hasn't reached out across this. I've no right to be angry. I've no right to feel anything. just continue. I'm pinching its nose and blowing breath into its lungs. have the eyelids moved ever so slightly or have I just imagined it. is it bouncing around in the darkness in there. it's hard for him to admit. she's never done anything on her own. what does that make me. now what'll he be like. how'll we contain him. enemies I've yet to meet. ones who frighten easily. what's he doing out there.

195

It's cluttered but the window's letting in a soft breeze. he's comfortable. he's alone. only sounds that he's accustomed to. he's dry. he's putting it down. he's disappointed. now what do I do. what do I owe him. my only hope is that she'll attribute my rudeness and desperation to this. something she may have helped to cause. by comparison is mild. above some. below others. but nothing we couldn't leave behind. dismissed with a wave. unseen and evaporating. after all nothing sticks in her head. like watching a sink drain. I'm trying too hard. if she can be wooed. I'll express this. I'll explain it to her. why I act on impulse. let it dictate my steps. then days afterward. waiting in line for something. doing some mindless task. I'll never want anything again. I won't even look. cave in on myself. why should I stop there. every one of them is just as guilty. and if they've succeeded. someone somewhere suffering. going over it again in his head. but I'll do nothing. it's out of my hands. when we're pressed together. when I'm trapped and have to listen to one of them talk. who's he to pity anyone. the possibilities are endless. ways to live one's life. it's just this moment. right now. he's scraping the grime off. they'd be corrupted. they'd forget how it felt. they'd insist that it somehow still applied. at least amongst each other. sitting around some makeshift table. a fitting end. without consequence. I can hit and he won't strike back. I can insult him and he'll pretend he wasn't listening. or he's lost in thought. or he's somehow reached immunity. but it's burning in there like a drop of poison. next time around. when we've shifted again. he asked for this. never gives anything in return. I'm through. I've seen what he's capable of. looks that pass between us. we're the only ones left. I'd take the blame if it meant that for a few hours we could see eye to eye. if she could give in. but she'll leave at once. I finally know what I need to say. every last word.

196

Every few months or so she's drawn in and then she's trapped. where everything that drives her comes from. the source. the same smells and warmth. it steadies her. they're playing house. there's no future. sips hesitantly. there's nothing left here. no forgiveness or need to be forgiven. no fear of being caught off guard. it's simply early in the afternoon. and chilly. his place is drafty. his hand's so much bigger than hers. like a nut in a shell inside his. what real harm has he done. with him they've always let things slide. it's bright. the dust is visible as it floats downward. settling around us. he's speaking. it doesn't matter. something that's crept in. a new way of looking at things. she remembers how this used to worry her. now it's only toys she'll have to pick up and put away. she's imagining him old. his eyes are the same. it's past us. not a shred of it remains. it felt like I was gone for years. he never comments on how the birds chirp. even when they're at their loudest. like it's always just only him in the world. I shape this as acceptance. I loosen my tongue. maybe someday we can take things more seriously. I must be destined for something. be it joy or misery. I just want it to begin. an empty space into which my belongings can fit. either way. I'm not afraid. what rattles the door from the outside. I'm hoping the lock gives. perhaps no one listens. I'd like to feel pride at times. for anything. something I've done. work continues as always. some people quit. no one ever feels they belong here. the construction slows everything to a crawl. she turns and leaves. I've stolen her soul in this short time. he said we'd never forget this. but we all have. what choice do we have if we want assurance. I can't control it. like blood gushing from a wound. I'm a failure. as I wake. as I wash my face. I carry this knowledge within me. it's a secret from her. I choose a seat on the train. I'm obvious. the least threatening person alive.

197

Still not an echo. people are selfish. I can wait forever. I can place him with the others. it isn't important. what carries me homewards when I'm lost. so many things we'll never do together. how I could've helped him out. everything's distorted. I live in the past. as useless as a fantasy. I've been left here. I'm walking through the train station wondering if I'm the only one that's real. if the rest aren't made of clay. or merely visions. she's too innocent. she shouldn't have come. it's exactly what they hope for. no one obeys the laws. if this exists then a thread must run through all of it. even the least likely. the ones who never flinch. a loss we all suffer. enticing even now. look where it's gotten him. I'd thought myself unique in this way. not chained to them. everyone's is new but mine has holes in it. the only memory I have of him. returning with nothing. how does it make him feel. but something can be wrung from this. my head down for now 'til they're at last upon me. an annoyance. an intrusion. what may break the spell. they're walking home together making each other laugh. I can do this. it's as easy as breathing. sitting in one place long enough. thank him for me. it's over and through. now lifeless again. as door nails. as stumps. they arrive like flies. as if no time had passed and we should never not expect them. if he had made any sense of it. if he had understood the meaning then dismissed it all as worthless she'd have crawled away and hid. but he's old and he was lost. to be expected after years of this. it's much better the second time. I wish I could be there. I wish she wasn't in the way. something I'd forgotten. the only way for these things to coexist. who's carrying what around. someday I'll turn in another direction. I think I hear her waking and approaching. she'll enter and the entire universe will change. I'm finally finished. I want to celebrate. I have to get dressed and go to work.

About the Author

David F. Hoenigman was born and raised in Cleveland, Ohio, but has lived in Tokyo, Japan since 1998. He is the organizer of Tokyo's bimonthly PAINT YOUR TEETH, a celebration of experimental music, literature and dance. Hoenigman regularly interviews avant-garde writers for the online journal *Word Riot*. He is currently working on his second novel, *Squeal For Joy*, forthcoming from Jaded Ibis Press.

Related links:
www.myspace.com/paintyourteeth
www.3ammagazine.com/3am/a-genuine-enslavement-of-the-attention
www.wordriot.org

About the Artist

Yasutoshi Yoshida is an Extreme Music composer and founder of the music label XERXES, currently living in Tokyo, Japan. His artwork grew out of album covers he created for his Hard Noise project, "Government Alpha," that was begun in 1994. With no formal training, Yoshida searched for an art method that would reflect his "Art-Brut" influences, resulting in collages that suggest the aggressive confluence of his sound compositions. See related links for selected discography:

Related links:
www.myspace.com/xerxes1969
www.geocities.jp/xerxes_alpha2001/